The Spice of Life

The Transformation

Jake Furie Lapin

Blackman Morgan Sachs Group
Jake Furie Lapin
PO Box 7503
Freehold, NJ 07728
www.tsolbook.com

Authors's Note: This is a work of fiction. Names, characters, places, and incidents are a product of the author's imagination. Locales and public names are sometimes used for atmospheric purposes. Any resemblance to actual people, living or dead, or to businesses, companies, events, institutions, or locales is completely coincidental.

Please direct media inquiries and event booking requests to
HANNA@BMSACHS.COM

The Spice of Life: The Transformation/ Jake Furie Lapin

ISBN 978-1499145342

DEDICATION

To my one and only child, Jacob. It's finally done. Love you.

ACKNOWLEDGMENTS

First and foremost, I must thank my parents, Fifi and Nabeel, who have sustained and supported me so much throughout my youth and even today as a man. To my son, Jacob, to whom my character takes his first name after, who has stood with me in the last few years in the writing and marketing of this book. To my fans and friends, who helped me during my trying years without expectation of anything in return. To my "The Spice of Life Vixens," better known as TSOLVixens in both my Twitter and Facebook Street Team, who hung in there with me during my ups and downs while writing this book, supported not only the project but myself as an author, and kept the faith and the message. To my awesome amazing inside supporters of this project, who carried me emotionally and financially to the project completion. To the REAL HazelEyed Vixen, who bore my first child and made me believe that I truly won't live my life alone, even though our marriage didn't work out as planned.

PRELUDE

I started this journey more out of a sense of curiosity
A need to understand and know what journeys I've been missing
The cab was crude, strong, and gentle, big and slow
The first few journeys were lessons learned; I felt new, unseasoned, abused, and misguided
But I was willing to keep driving, as I quickly learned I liked the adventures
And that each journey was special, unique, and I wanted more

I refined the cab: new headlights, slimmer body to attract better passengers
Same engine, same pump, better premium gas
I defined the cab ride: Creative partners, Amazing lovers, or Best of friends
And it's OK if you don't know what ride you want, or you may want them all
Don't be scared, as being scared is usually the ride to take
I am your driver, I'll always be there
Just feed the meter, even if it's just aimless

I apologize if our ride ends short, as I may have felt that our journey was over
Don't try to understand the driver, as to understand, I need to know as well
But if you enjoy our ride, and if you are unsure of our destination,

Just keep feeding the meter; otherwise, I'll run out of gas

Occasionally I may ask for other passengers to share the ride, as we
have a mutual journey
Or you may want to wear the belt, the tighter the better
We can even swap, and I'll watch you drive
It might be necessary to take a short break and stop, and I'll wait,
your driver
Just keep feeding the meter, so I know to keep waiting

However, if I feel ditched, I'll be disappointed and feel cheated
I would rather you pay your fare, even if you have no money
Just don't pay with three dollar bills or ask me for a discount, as I
gave you my cab
And it's OK if you found a better cab, just pay your fare along with
mine
You can kick the tires, slam the door, and give the cab dents
The pain is superficial, temporary, and easily fixed
The engine and pump are unique, and irreplaceable
That pain is real and permanent, not so easily fixed
The cabbie will retire, when there is no one left to feed the meter

{ 1 }

The morning light broke, pushing incessantly through half-closed blinds. Kelli moaned in her sleep. *He was fucking her. Her entire body was alive with pleasure and she was close to cumming, hard. He had her arms pinned over her head, thrusting fully into her, with her naked legs thrown over his shoulders. She lifted her entire body to take him fully. God, it felt good. So incredibly good. His cock must be absolutely huge; her whole pussy was full of him. She was almost there, straining against him to reach her climax. He grabbed her hand, put her fingers in his mouth, and began sucking on them. Suddenly he started to lap at the top of her hand with his tongue. Unsure why he was spending so much time there, Kelli was becoming annoyed. It started to feel strange. Why was his tongue so sloppy? Where was her orgasm? What was...what...?*

Her eyes popped open. Immediately jerking her hand off the bed, where it lay on top of the sheets, she found her golden retriever, Samson, looking up at her from the side of the bed with his big wet nose and tongue. Her hand was covered in his drool. "Oh my god! Gross, Samson!" Kelli groaned. "Ewwwwww." She pushed Samson away and rolled over, feeling disgusted, but the atmosphere of the sex dream was still with her.

She closed her eyes and tried to remember the face of the man who was fucking her, but it was just a shadow. Someone she'd never even met. Even as she tried to recall the details, the dream disappeared.

Ugh, she thought. *Forget about it. Better get up.* Even before she rose to check, she knew that the day outside was hard, cold, and bright. She groaned inwardly. Not even any snow. Snow would have made today just a little bit easier.

She turned from the window, just in time to see Paul twitch and let out a snort in his sleep. Gazing at her husband of twenty-two years, she saw his slack, open mouth, the spot of dried spittle on his stubbled cheek, and the flannel pajamas she had been trying to convince him to throw away for years. Looking at him, a familiar thought came: *He looks ridiculous.* Immediately following that thought was the equally familiar pang of guilt and ache of loneliness. *Maybe we can make a new start this year.* She made another mental note to talk to Paul about New Year's Eve and fresh beginnings.

It was early still, too early to call either of the girls, so Kelli went downstairs to make coffee. The tree lights were on; she hadn't had the heart to turn them off before bed. They winked at her, reminding her of all those Christmases with Kaitlyn and Simone. The girls used to wake them up at 6:00 a.m., or earlier, especially when they were really small. Paul and Kelli would be dragged out of bed to stumble down in their bathrobes, exhausted from late-night gift-wrapping and glasses of eggnog, while their daughters squealed with delight and tore open stockings and gifts. As the girls became teenagers, they slept in much later, but there was still always an air of excitement and anticipation in the house on Christmas morning.

This morning, however, barely felt like Christmas at all. With both children gone for the first time, the emptiness in the house was palpable. Kelli sipped her coffee listlessly and gazed at the gifts under the tree. *Definitely a smaller pile than usual*, she thought. Her eldest daughter, Kaitlyn, was happily settled in California, where she had landed last year after graduating from UC Berkeley with a degree in social work. Simone, Kelli's youngest, was a sophomore at Columbia, but was currently traveling in Europe. Kelli had mailed all of Kaitlyn's presents to her in California, but the gifts for Simone were still here. They had discussed it, and decided that it made more sense for Simone to open them when she returned from her law firm internship in the spring. Kelli had pressed her youngest daughter, "Don't you want something now? Let me send you one or two little gifts, at least!"

But Simone had been adamant, "It's fine, Mom," she said. "Honestly! I'm going to be in Biarritz for Christmas, and presents would just get in the way. That is, if they even made it here on time." Kelli felt mildly hurt, but she let it go. That was one thing about being a therapist: One learned how to let go. Actually doing it, however, could be a whole other matter.

Her thoughts once again turned to Paul. They had agreed to take it easy on the gifts for each other this year. Not that it really made a difference; Paul had never really been a great gift-giver, even in the early days of their marriage. He had made an effort for a long time, though. She had to give him that. On a couple of occasions, he had even gotten it right: a beautiful silk scarf one year, or a bottle of her favorite perfume. But things had changed lately, and it had become increasingly impossible to mask her disappointment at opening up yet another set of towels or photo frames. She knew he tried, but she couldn't help but wonder if he really had so little sense of what she enjoyed or needed. Eventually, his gifts to her trickled to almost nothing: a token bottle of hand lotion or a pair of gloves. After decades, she'd almost convinced herself that she accepted this part of him, but there was still that tiny sting every Christmas, every birthday, every anniversary. Yesterday, on Christmas Eve, they decided to get the whole thing over with and had opened each other's gifts. She had bought him the latest tablet, and he had bought her a set of new copper-bottomed pots and pans. She wasn't even surprised. She didn't like to cook—never had—but whatever. It was just another reflection of the state of their relationship.

New Year's, that's what they needed to discuss. She had been dreading the conversation, but she knew it had to happen. There couldn't be a repeat of last year. She cringed, thinking back to the previous January. She had made such an effort. She'd had her hair done in the way that Paul had always liked since they'd been in high school: long and wavy, with subtle highlights. She had gone for a mani/pedi, and had even gotten a Brazilian wax—something Kaitlyn and Simone had been after her to do for years. She had always been afraid to try waxing, because she'd always had a full bush of pubic hair and knew it would hurt, but surprisingly, it had been rather clean and enjoyable. She loved the feel of her bare skin between her legs. Coming home from the wax, she became aroused and wet in anticipation of things to come. She'd bought a new dress: a sexy, burgundy, cocktail number that flattered her figure without being too revealing. After all, her figure was still something to be showcased. She knew this, and was quietly satisfied, although she recognized that good luck had a part to play. If it weren't for her father's side of the family, with their long legs and racing metabolism, it might be a different story. She smiled, thinking of all the times she'd gone out running with her dad. It had paid off in giving her a sleek, long-lasting figure.

In any case, she had looked and felt fantastic last New Year's Eve. People noticed, too. They had gone to dinner at the Howells' apartment, and all night she felt approving male eyes on her. Jeff Thomas had even started flirting openly and clumsily towards the end of the evening, after he'd had far too many drinks. She'd had a few glasses of wine herself, but she was focused on Paul. It had been a good night for him; he'd been at his best: gregarious, witty, and charming. He looked nice, too, with the new shirt she'd bought him for Christmas that year. It almost felt like the old days. She had worried that he would overdo it with the vodka again, but he seemed to pace himself better than usual.

After midnight, just before their taxi arrived to take them home from the party, she'd found him alone in the kitchen. Putting her arms around her husband's neck, she pressed up against him, nibbled his earlobe, and whispered, "I want you to take me tonight, babe. I need you. I need to be with you." He'd smiled and responded to her kiss, briefly, before they were interrupted by Andrea Conte, who was looking for some more crackers. The kiss gave her hope, though, and in the taxi she'd even gone so far as to cuddle up next to him and slip her hand up and down his inner thigh. No reaction. He had either ignored it, or was too drunk to notice.

When they arrived home, she went into the kitchen for a glass of water and came back to find Paul passed out on the bed wearing just his underwear and socks. Her heart sank, but still, she tried to rouse him. She even ran her hand over the soft bulge in his briefs, hoping beyond hope for some response. Nothing. He was dead to the world. So the night ended with Kelli sitting alone in the dark living room, wearing her sexy dress and gazing out the window at the streetlights. She sipped her water and tried not to cry, but the familiar tears came in the end, nonetheless.

What a way to bring in the New Year. Worse, it had set the tone for the next twelve months. Kelli winced and tried to count up the number of times that she and her husband had been intimate since then. After the New Year's party, there had been one time in mid-January, in part because Paul felt guilty, she suspected. Then the day after her birthday in April—Paul had been too drunk on her actual birthday, twice while on a three-week vacation in Mexico in July, and one random night in November, when she had to practically beg him.

What a joke, she thought for the thousandth time. *I spend every day at work trying to help my clients have satisfying sex lives, and here I am, stuck with Paul. The sexless sex therapist. Great!*

The phone rang, startling Kelli out of her reverie. The connection was faint and crackly, as Simone's voice came from the other end. "Just wanted to call and say Merry Christmas to you and Dad," she shouted. "I'm about to go out for lunch on the Champs-Élysées." She sounded bright and distant, and cut the conversation short after just a few minutes.

"Call again soon, hon!" Kelli told her, but Simone had already hung up the phone. She pictured her beautiful, blonde, nineteen-year-old daughter and felt a strong pang of loss from missing her. She then thought of Kaitlyn—tall, strong Kaitlyn—and her current boyfriend, Greg. They would still be fast asleep in California; there was no doubt they would call later in the day.

When Paul stumbled downstairs a few minutes later, he was angry with her for not waking him. "My youngest daughter calls from France, on Christmas Day, and you don't get me out of bed to wish her a happy holiday?" he grumbled.
Kelli shrugged. "You were still sleeping; I figured you needed it." She held back from adding that if she had tried to wake him, her efforts would have been met with intense resistance.

"Well, what about Kaitlyn?"

"Haven't heard from her, yet. I'm sure that she and Greg are still asleep. You know how it is. We'll try them in a while."

There was a pause. She gazed at her stocky, barrel-chested, brown-eyed husband, and mustered up her courage. "Paul, there is something I want to talk to you about."

"Jesus, Kelli! I just woke up five minutes ago, and it's Christmas morning! Can you give me a break? Does it have to be right now?"

She felt irritation rise from where it lurked beneath the surface these days, always threatening to come out and sabotage her interactions with Paul. She drew in a deep, calming breath and tried to keep her tone neutral. "I just wanted to ask you something. It doesn't have to be a big deal. Can we talk about it now, before we get distracted? It's really important to me."

He groaned and rolled his eyes. It still amazed her sometimes how childish he really was. "Fine. What is it?"

She sat down across from him at the breakfast bar and paused for a moment, gathering her courage and her thoughts. "So, you know how we're going to the Howells' party again on New Year's Eve?"

"Yeah," he grunted.

"Well, I just wanted to say that, uh, well, do you remember what

8

happened last year?"

Paul's eyebrows shot up, and he ran his hand nervously through his thinning brown hair. "I remember that we had a moderately good time and came home. Was there something I missed?"

"Maybe. Do you remember how...how I told you last year at the party that I wanted to make love when we got home?"

Mild surprise changed to complete bewilderment on Paul's face. "How you came on to me at the party, before we left? Yeah, I kinda remember. I was pretty wasted. But what does that have to do with anything?"

Kelli felt her composure slipping a little, and her words came out in a rush. "Paul, the thing is...it was really important to me to have us bring in the New Year with intimacy. Maybe it's partly my fault; I should have expressed it more clearly at the time, instead of just trying to seduce you like that. But what I'm trying to say is, I really needed you that night, and it, uh, it didn't happen. So I wanted to talk to you this year because I just really don't want a repeat of last year. I want to have sex on New Year's Eve when we get home. I need us to make love, as husband and wife. OK? Can we do that? Can we please just do that?"

Paul's face softened and he grinned that crooked grin of his. "Aww, Kellikins! You're so goddamn cute sometimes, you know that? Of course we can fuck on New Year's Eve. I wouldn't miss it for the world!"

Fuck? Kelli thought. *I can easily fuck with a vibrator. I wanted to make love. He just doesn't get it.* Paul came around the bar and wrapped her up in a familiar bear hug. She could feel his heart beating through his bathrobe. It made her feel sick and furious all at the same time. She pushed him back, away from her. "You just don't get it, do you?" she asked him. She could feel herself glaring. "Do you realize it has been months since we fucked? MONTHS!? Do you even care?"

Paul stared at her blankly. Then he shrugged. "Things are fine," he said. "Anyway, whatever. Yeah, we'll fuck on New Year's Eve. Happy now?"

Kelli felt her anger turning into despair. "Sure," she mumbled. "Yeah. Really happy." She stared down at her hands, and then turned to the cupboard to take out a glass. She wasn't really thirsty, but it gave her a reason to turn her back to him.

Paul didn't seem to notice. "I'm going to watch some TV, OK?" her husband called, walking through to the living room. So that was that. The conversation was over. Kelli felt weak. Relief coupled with an underlying sense of desperation. How like Paul to react like that. Just smooth things over and pretend nothing ever happened...yes, that was her husband. This wasn't the first time she'd raised the intimacy issue with him, but the reaction was always the same. He acted as though she had said something really obvious, usually hugged her, and then nothing changed.

She couldn't let it go though. Her gut told her that pushing the issue would be a mistake, but the frustration was too great to hold back. She moved to the living room and stood in the doorway. Paul had flipped on the TV, and *It's a Wonderful Life* was playing. Somehow that fact made Kelli feel even more helpless and infuriated.

"Paul."

"Uh huh?"

"I know this isn't easy for either of us. But just now I didn't feel like you really listened, or understood what I was saying. It's just that...well, you know...I guess I'll just say it. Our love life hasn't been too good lately. I would like for that to change. I'd also like to feel like my feelings are validated."

Silence from the armchair. Paul stared at the TV but she could tell he had tensed up.

"Paul? Can we talk about this? Please?"

Without a word, Paul stood up and walked right past her out of the room. Kelli called after him.

"Where are you going, Paul? Can we just talk?

Paul turned on the stairs and faced her. "You know I hate this fucking therapist shit, Kelli! I really hate it. There is no problem with us or our sex life. I'm fine. And you would be too, if you weren't such a condescending bitch all the time!" He turned again and soon Kelli heard the bedroom door slam.

And there it was. The conversation was over, just like that. Typical.

Wow. So this is how bad it's become, she thought. *I knew it was bad, but I feel like I've been in denial.* She didn't want to force Paul into a full-blown fight; she knew that it wouldn't work and would just cause him to shut down. She couldn't help but think of Brenda, one of her past clients. For years, Brenda had existed in a sexless marriage; it had completely sapped her of her self-esteem and sense of worth. Kelli had advised her to leave over and over again. *I've become Brenda.* The thought filled her with horror. *This New Year's Eve is going to make or break us.* As soon as the idea entered her mind, she knew it was true. Feeling forlorn and defeated, Kelli made her way to the deserted living room, and sat down in front of the TV, just in time to watch a black-and-white George Bailey crash his car into a snow-covered tree.

The New Year's Eve party was an annual event. Carmelo Conte was a former colleague of Paul's who had worked with him in the garbage collection business. His wife, Andrea, was a petite, dyed-blonde socialite who tottered around on huge platform heels and talked far too loudly. Kelli had never really liked Andrea; she found her chatter to be vapid and meaningless. But out of courtesy she sipped her champagne and nodded while Andrea talked about her miniature poodle and her new pair of Manolo Blahniks. She hated these parties; everyone was so crude, and she knew that several guests were involved in the mob. She was very uncomfortable and the heavy drinking didn't help.

Eventually, Andrea wandered off and Kelli made her way to the bar for a refill. She felt male eyes on her as she passed. As usual, she looked fantastic. She'd chosen a strapless, green, silk sheath dress that was just long enough to be elegant, but short enough to show off her legs. It was a dress that Paul loved, or at least used to love. Earlier in the evening, she had carefully selected it from her closet, along with some strappy, green, Louboutin stiletto heels. She also had put more care than usual into applying her makeup, choosing a shade of dark, smoky, burnt-gold eye shadow that perfectly complemented her green eyes, and a luscious shade of red lipstick. She'd worn the gold and diamond drop earrings that she had inherited from her mother, and had even taken more time than usual to carefully curl the thick auburn hair that was her pride and joy. She had finished it off with her favorite necklace: a sapphire pendant. As she walked, she knew that she was inspiring lust in the men around her, but the thought gave her no pleasure. She was all too aware that she would be going home with Paul to a cold bed, yet again. She had worked so hard to look gorgeous for him, hoping that it would ignite something, but like everything else she'd tried, it didn't seem to be working.

At the bar, she felt someone sit down beside her. "Kelli, isn't it?" She turned and saw Carlos Mitchell. They'd met a couple of years earlier at a work function. Carlos was older, in his early 60s, but he was a handsome man, with salt-and-pepper hair and strong shoulders.

She smiled invitingly. "Well hiiiii! It's been a while! How are you, Carlos?" She saw his approving glance skim over her trim body and tight dress.

"I'm just fine...and I must say, you're looking scrumptious, Kelli."

It occurred to her in that moment that she could have Carlos, if she wanted him. She saw the hunger in his eyes and knew that it matched her own. She'd heard through the grapevine that he was newly divorced, and for the first time, Kelli didn't suppress the thoughts that rose in her mind. *Yes, I could have Carlos. Maybe even right now.* She could flirt for a while, have a few more drinks, and then they could just slip away into one of the empty adjoining rooms, or maybe even FUCK in the bathroom. *Take that, Paul.* She could run her hands over his tall, strong body and feel him come alive to her...feel his manhood harden in response and preparation. Then she'd let him roughly push her down to the ground, hike up her green dress, and she would draw his mouth down to taste how incredibly wet she was, how very eager...it was a delicious, forbidden thought.

Kelli suddenly came to her senses. *What was she doing?* She smiled back at Carlos and suddenly felt slightly disgusted with herself. No, that wasn't hunger in his eyes. He was just being friendly and polite, making conversation. Feeling unsettled, she politely excused herself and sought refuge with the wives of some executives who had gathered in another corner of the room. She looked around for Paul and saw him talking to some of the more slutty women in the room, the ones with too much makeup and ultra-low-cut tops. He clearly was not missing her. He barely even looked up from the skanky brunette to whom he was talking.

That's typical. Kelli felt disgusted yet again. She remembered a previous party where Paul had gone off with some of the guys and hadn't even bothered to tell her. She'd been worried sick and finally went home without him. She was just about to call the police in the early hours of the morning when he finally stumbled into the door, drunk. It turned out that he had stayed out drinking with his buddies the whole time. He never even apologized.

On the way home, Paul was predictably drunk. He could barely string a sentence together and passed out on the passenger side of the cab's back seat. Kelli couldn't stop thinking about that moment with Carlos. What had she been thinking, letting her thoughts go down that road? She'd actually considered cheating on Paul. She was pondering this when suddenly she became aware of the radio in the cab. The cab driver had gone to turn the radio off when Kelli and Paul got in, but she'd told him to leave it on. She needed some kind of white noise to fill up the emptiness. But what was playing right now?

....for married people who simply aren't getting what they need, crave, and desire, www.tsol.xxx offers a way to meet like-minded people who seek discreet, intimate encounters. Bored or unhappy at home, but unwilling to leave? Tsol.xxx understands the complications. Have the best of both worlds! There's no reason to suffer alone, when you can find sexual and emotional healing with someone in a similar situation. Create your free profile at www.tsol.xxx.

Kelli was suddenly wide awake. *Online dating for an affair?* She had several friends who had navigated the online dating world with varying degrees of success, but it had never occurred to her that websites might exist to help people have affairs. She turned and looked at Paul slumped against the opposite window. Like a cold, hard slap in the face, it came to her that even if he hadn't been drunk, she still didn't really want to have sex with him. She hadn't felt attracted to him in that way in a long time—years, even. The spark was gone. It felt outrageous to admit it, but she knew it was true. *An affair. I could actually have an affair.* Suddenly, Kelli couldn't wait to get home.

Kelli managed to wake Paul up enough for her to get him out of the cab. The cabbie helped her get him up the stairs and onto the bed. Once he was sprawled out, snoring, she thanked the cabbie for his help. He had been gazing into her eyes, and also down at the sapphire pendant she was wearing. He had very striking green eyes, but Kelli was too exhausted to register anything else. She paid him and headed to the living room to boot up her laptop. She couldn't really believe that she was doing this, but it felt exciting. It even felt right. She typed in the web address she'd heard in the cab. When the website came up, it looked classy, simple, and discrete, which was somehow reassuring.

At first, she tried to browse the profiles of male users, but the site would not allow access to photos. So, following the online instructions, Kelli began to establish her own profile.

Appearance: *red hair, green eyes, 5'8", slender*

My best physical assets: That was an easy one. *legs, butt, long hair*

About me:

Kelli paused. *How does one describe oneself without sounding either arrogant or ridiculous?* Finally, she wrote:

About me: *I am looking to love and be loved, without changing our current situation, and to explore all of life's possibilities. Life is too short to be wasted...I'm tired of waiting for change that will never come. I need to create my own change.*

Interests: *long walks, good books, close friends.*

God, she thought. *Could I sound any more boring and clichéd?* She erased what she'd written and started over.

Interests: *Discovering life's little pleasures, loving, and being loved. Going deeper. Creating and maintaining adventures.*

Not great, but better. She moved on to the next section.

What I'm looking for in a partner:

What am I looking for? She wasn't even sure. Was it just the idea of having some great sex that excited her? Or was it the possibility of actually having a real connection again, after all this time? She'd had it with Paul a very long time ago. It had faded away over the years, but yes, it had been there once. She craved that closeness, that melding of mind, body, and spirit. But how do you put that into words?

Finally, she wrote: *Someone who knows what it's like to be with someone, but alone. Someone who wants to explore the limits of connection, in every sense: spiritual, physical, and emotional.*

A little cheesy maybe, but it was true.

There was one last section to complete.

What turns you on?

There was a list of bullets that could be selected. Some of them were quite explicit and Kelli felt a rush of pleasure as she selected a few.

- Sensual massage
- Giving oral sex
- Receiving oral sex
- Role play
- Dressing up/Lingerie
- Aggressive/Take-Charge nature
- Confidence
- Good sense of humor
- Fit/Muscular body

Kelli looked at the list. *Was there anything else?* She briefly hesitated, and then added one more:

- Light, kinky fun

She remembered how, in the early days of their relationship, she had tried to get Paul to sexually experiment. She had fantasized about having him tie her up and forcefully explore her body with his mouth, so she bought a pair of fuzzy handcuffs. Paul had acted somehow offended, and ultimately had refused to use them. The handcuffs ended up gathering dust in a closet for years. Eventually, when they'd moved, Kelli had found them and ended up throwing them away. At that point, she didn't want to be reminded of the sexual excitement she was missing.

Now for the photos. Kelli opened up a few albums on her computer and selected a range of photos: one with her in a bikini, taken in Maui last year; another from a work conference in London, in which she was wearing a tailored suit; and a third photo with her smiling wide and holding up her favorite drink, a dirty martini with bleu-cheese-stuffed olives. That would do for now. She was poised to upload them, but hesitated. *Who knew who was out there? What if someone she knew saw her?*

On second thought, she decided to upload these photos to the "secret photos" area of the site. She added one photo that was taken from behind, as she walked along the beach at sunset. It didn't show her face, but it did show off her long auburn hair, as well as her legs and shapely ass. *Yes, that would do nicely.* For her public profile picture, she finally chose a photo and cropped it into a body shot that showed her from the neck down in one of her favorite dresses, an emerald green, satin cocktail number. She was wearing her favorite necklace, a white gold pendant with a sapphire. *Yes, that's nice. Gives them a good taste.*

With her profile complete, her finger hovered over the mouse, as she contemplated the "Submit" button on the profile. Was she ready?

What the hell? she thought. *It's not like I actually have to do anything. I'll just see what happens.*

She pressed "Submit", shut down the computer, and went to bed.

The next morning, Kelli eagerly booted up the computer and visited the website. She had expected to find one or two messages, so she was dumbfounded to see that her inbox contained sixty new emails. *Wow*, she thought. *I'm not alone?*

She opened the first one. The subject line read, "Hi." The body of the email contained one line. The member profile showed that the guy was 6'2" and 280 lbs.

ur sexy. wanna chat?

Kelli winced, and hit "Delete." The next message had no subject line at all and read:

Nice legs. If you are up for a hot time and a phat dick, hit me up. Five-oh-five seven two nine, 6 four one.

This did not bode well. As Kelli skimmed through the remainder of the messages, most contained photos, some very explicit, and she quickly weeded most of them out. There were two normal-appearing emails, but the photos that the first sender included showed him with a beer gut, black leather jacket, and a scraggly goatee. The second guy didn't have any profile photos at all and sounded incredibly dull. Kelli sighed. Maybe this was just a bad idea. None of these people were even remotely suitable, and it was clear that the majority hadn't even bothered to read her own profile.

She continued to check her mail throughout the day, and was amazed to find that the messages kept rolling in like clockwork. It seemed that each time she logged in, there were five or ten new emails. One of the messages had the subject "Check this out" and an attachment. Out of morbid curiosity, Kelli opened the attachment and was unwillingly rewarded for her efforts with a photo of a man's naked, erect penis. She was not the slightest bit aroused by the sight of a stranger's genitalia, but did find it intriguing. She cast a critical, curious eye over the phallus and noted the size and shape. *Meh. Kind of crooked. Big enough, I suppose, but who cares?* The man who sent it didn't have a word to say for himself, so she didn't even bother with a courtesy reply.

She began to feel very bored with the messages she was receiving and decided to browse on her own. Most of the profiles didn't have photos so she skipped over those. *Not really fair*, she thought, given the fact that she herself chose not to post many photos, but still. She wanted to know what she was getting into. She couldn't believe how bad some of the profiles were. Few men bothered to write much about themselves, and the photo selection was even more disappointing.

There was the guy who said he was 45, but looked much closer to 65. There were a large number of photos where the man had snapped his own pic with a smart phone, showing a bare chest in the mirror from the neck down. Most were less than impressive. And there were the stoic guys who stared straight into the camera without cracking even a glimmer of a smile; these reminded her of prison mug shots. She was almost amused. *Photos of you and your wife/girlfriend? Really? You and your cat is very disturbing. You in a boat with a beer gut holding up a beer is NOT attractive. Uggghhh. Nice cock; wish the rest of you was just as good.*

There were a handful of handsome, attractive men, though. She found a few who caught her eye and read their profiles, but nothing really jumped out at her. It was all pretty generic. *What am I even looking for?* she wondered. *What would feel right?*

This went on for a day or two, and then it came: midweek. She was nursing a cup of coffee and nibbling on some toast when she opened up her inbox. There was a message from a user she hadn't seen before: EnjoyLifeNJ. There was black and white photo of a man in a mask, with charcoal effect. She almost hit delete but stopped:

Hello there beautiful

This may come as a surprise to you, but I am writing to you without attaching a cock shot. I couldn't help but be drawn to what you wrote in describing yourself. You are right in what you said about creating change. I, too, am seeking the most out of life. Life is for living. I know that when I was younger I was naturally full of enthusiasm, passion, and adventure. Were you? How do we ever lose that? It doesn't have to stay lost...I've been on a journey over the past few years and I can assure you that all the joy, all the juice, and all the fire in life is still there. We just need to reach out and take it.

I can help you find that again. I've learned some incredible lessons, and I'd like the opportunity to share these lessons. I'd like to teach you. You can wake up again...all it takes is the right touch to stir those coals that I sense are smoldering within you.

Will you meet me for a drink? La Dolce Vita in Soho is one of my favorite places to enjoy getting to know someone. How about Friday night?

P.S. I enjoyed looking at your beautiful bust and necklace, and I hope the rest of you is just as nice.

EnjoyLifeNJ

Kelli was intrigued. There was something in the tone of the message that caught her, hooked her. The juice, the joy, the fire...Yes. That resonated deeply. Until now, she had held back from communicating with anyone on the site, but this email called out for a response.

Hesitantly, feeling a thrill in her stomach, she clicked the reply button and began writing.

EnjoyLifeNJ ---

May I see your secret pics?

K.

Moments later, the reply came.

Dear K,

Here I reread your profile and thought you were into chemistry and passion. I spent quite some time writing to you in hopes we could have a conversation. If you believe that sex is more mental than physical; if you want to respect my discretion as I haven't asked for your secret pics; and if you truly believe that you can find the spark again, and not just have a one-night stand, then please tell me about yourself. If you want to just look for any hot guy and hope he doesn't use you, then please pass on...

J

Kelli was impressed. *Wow. That was direct and different. OK, he is right.* She responded:

J,

You're right; it did used to feel different. I feel like I've been lost at sea for a long time. The idea of recovering some sense of passion and adventure is very appealing to me.

Tell me a little more about this journey. How did it begin?

K

The reply came within minutes.

K,

My journey began when I realized that life is too precious and too beautiful to spend being unhappy. So I stopped being unhappy. I started taking what I want.

You can stop being unhappy too. There are ways to be more alive than you've ever been.

Meet me at La Dolce Vita. No pressure, no strings. I would like to offer you your first lesson, that's all. They have a great, lively happy hour crowd on Thursday nights. Great mixer, great music, and a nice place to unwind.

J

Kelli was torn. After thinking for a moment or two, she wrote:

You aren't some sort of kinky pervert, are you?

The reply was almost immediate:

Kinky is a relative word, and without knowing what your sexual tastes are, I cannot say. What seems kinky the first time may be incredibly enjoyable the next.

J

Meeting someone was obviously the next step in this process, but it meant that she was really serious about pursuing an affair. She decided not to reply right away. Better to think about it for a day or two.

Over the next 48 hours, Kelli kept playing out scenarios in her mind. In one version of events, she met up with this man and it ended in complete disaster. Paul would find out, the girls would never forgive her…her marriage and life as she knew it would be turned upside down and ruined. But in a second version, the one she kept returning to, it was very different. In this fantasy, she met EnjoyLifeNJ— whatever his real name may be—and embarked on a passionate, intense, and satisfying affair. She imagined where they would meet...at hotels? His place? Certainly not hers. But in any case, he would gather her up and touch her, all over her body, fill her up. She felt a thrill of pleasure run between her legs at the thought. She needed satisfaction; her sexual frustration was becoming unbearable. The emptiness inside of her needed to experience raw masculinity, overpowering her, thrusting into her.

Eventually, the fantasy overcame her, and she found herself back in front of the computer, looking at her online profile.

Dear EnjoyLifeNJ,

I am intrigued with the idea of this lesson you offer to teach me. I need a teacher like that.

I would like to meet. First, though, could you tell me your real name?

K

P.S. I've allowed you to have access to my secret pics. I think you'll like what you see...let me know.

Kelli pressed "send" and waited. And waited. Four hours later, she was checking from her office at work in between client sessions. Still no reply. Kelli was a little bit horrified at how obsessed she was becoming. Initially, she had checked her email every half an hour, but now she was checking at every possible opportunity. *C'mon*, she thought. *I made the leap. I said I would meet you...now where are you?*

By evening, when Kelli returned home from work, there was still no reply. She knew it was irrational of her to feel irritated, yet she was annoyed and frustrated. She had worked her way up to this and now it had stalled.

She considered writing again—just a line or two to check in—but quickly discarded the idea. It seemed far too attentive and needy.

The final straw came when it occurred to her to check and see if EnjoyLifeNJ had signed into the website. She checked and saw that he had indeed been online in the past 24 hours. *Why hasn't he replied?*

Kelli felt increasingly upset and annoyed. Her annoyance was the top layer of a deep sense of disappointment. None of this was really working out. She had known it would turn out like this. It had just been a foolish idea in the first place, doomed to fail. She was married to Paul, would stay married to Paul, and would suffer through the next two or three decades of a joyless, sexless, and dissatisfied existence. That was how it was. She wouldn't break the girls' hearts by leaving their father. She'd just stagnate, like old water in a pond.

ping Kelli jerked her head up and stared at the screen. That sound meant she had a new message. Yes, there was something in her mailbox! It must be EnjoyLifeNJ. She felt far too eager as she opened it. *Oh.* Her heart sank. It was a message from someone called Sexgod11 and read:

> *Your a real fox. I'd like to see if you're sexy tale is bushy and red to match your pretty hair.*

Ugh. Who ARE these people? This guy obviously had an IQ of 60. Kelli was done. She quickly went to the "Accounts" tab and selected "Disable/Delete account". Enough was enough.

{ 2 }

When Nina called, Kelli was thrilled to hear from her old friend. She had no idea that she was back in town. Nina had been in California for the past year or so, working as a banking recruiter. Kelli had seen her once or twice, but for the most part they were both busy with their lives.

Nina was one of Kelli's oldest friends. They had met the first week of their freshman year at high school and had been nearly inseparable. After graduation, Kelli and Paul had been struggling, especially with Kelli's pregnancy, and needed all the help they could get to pay the bills on their tiny apartment in Clinton, NJ. Kelli, Paul, and Nina decided to share the apartment while Nina pursued her career in marketing and sales, and Kelli continued to work her way through graduate school.

Nina was wild and always had been. She possessed a Marilyn Monroe figure with long, luscious, black curls, full features, and latte-colored skin. She had led Kelli through all kinds of crazy escapades. Once, Nina had suggested that they go out in Greenwich Village and bar hop while posing as obscure European royalty. She'd even come up with unique accents for each of them. Kelli had been Romanian and Nina, Croatian. They'd both drawn all kinds of attention to themselves; Nina absolutely soaked it up. Kelli enjoyed Nina's pranks but had always been content to enjoy them in tandem, and usually being the more sober of the two, she often rescued Nina from all sorts of compromising situations.

On the answering machine, Nina's message was typically enthusiastic:

"Kelli! My bodaciously beautiful goddess! How ARE you? I'm in New York for a few days. We really must go out. It's been far, far too long. I have so much to tell you! CALL ME!"

It was perfect timing. It had been a few days since Kelli abandoned her online adventure, and she'd felt morose and slightly depressed since then. Before she'd gone on the site, she was still able to convince herself that there was some kind of hope for her and Paul. But since she'd come clean with herself and realized that the spark was completely dead, her married life had become almost unbearable. She could hardly stand to be in the same room as Paul; even the scent of his body made her feel slightly sick to her stomach and grossed out overall. Not that he had tried to be near her or make any sexual advances. Nothing had changed in that department. Kelli was grateful for once. Instead, she'd turned to self-pleasuring, even more than usual. As she brought herself to orgasm in her bathtub, over and over, she fantasized about the nameless, masked man who had teased her so mercilessly and then disappeared. She had even given him a face of sorts, in her mind's eye. It was a composite of several ex-boyfriends, with a dose of George Clooney blended in. It worked pretty well. But even her sessions with her vibrator were growing stale.

A night out with Nina was just what she needed to relax and let loose a little. A few cocktails…talking about old times…yes, that sounded about right.

She picked up the phone and dialed Nina's number. Nina answered on the third ring, sounding breathless.

"Kelllllllliiiiiii! So good to hear from you, babe! I was starting to think I'd have to make my own fun without you. Not that being on my own ever held me back…," She chuckled her throaty laugh.

"Haha…I know, I know," laughed Kelli. "You've never been one to stay in on a Friday night, I know that! But seriously, Neens, I'm thrilled that you're in town. I am so ready for a good night out. Did you have anything in mind?"

"Me? Honey, you're the native here now. I was hoping you could suggest a place."

Kelli paused. There was a place that sprang to mind…

"So….there's always Thorne, in Kenil, on the New Jersey side. I know you like it there. Or we could go to Casellino, on 52nd. There's also this new cocktail lounge I've been wanting to try out. It's in Soho. It's called La Dolce Vita. Maybe we could check it out?"

For a second Kelli imagined that Nina hesitated, and her own heart skipped a beat. But then the reply came down the line.

"Thorne is definitely tempting, but I kinda want to get into Manhattan. Let's go to that Dolce Vita place. What time? And more importantly…what are you wearing?"

The two friends made plans to meet at 9 p.m. It was already a few minutes past seven o'clock, so Kelli jumped in the shower and then started getting dressed. With Nina's input, she had decided to wear her red wrap dress, the ruched one with the V neck, along with her favorite black Manolo Blahnik stiletto sandals. She added some tastefully dark eyeliner, put on some dangly, shimmery silver earrings, and let her hair cascade long and loose. At the last minute, she added her white gold square-shaped pendant with the sapphire. Looking in her full-length mirror, she felt a thrill of excitement.

She knew that it was silly to imagine that going to La Dolce Vita could possibly cause her to run into EnjoyLifeNJ, but still, the thought was in the back of her mind. And if she did happen to bump into him? Well, she'd show him! With how she looked tonight, he'd clearly see what he was missing, and would regret not having replied to her email. Ha! Revenge would be sweet. *He probably isn't even that good looking or charming in person*, she thought. *Probably just another fat, old douchebag.*

Kelli arrived at La Dolce Vita around 9:30 p.m. She entered the bar and saw Nina sitting at a small table, looking mildly disgruntled.

"I should have told you eight thirty, Kells! I forgot your habit of being chronically late." Nina gave a mock scowl and then embraced Kelli in a huge hug.

"I'm really sorry, Nina…I really am. You know how I just lose track of time. Forgive me?"

Nina's dark eyes danced and she gave a huge smile. "Of course, hon. Now what ARE we going to drink? Let's get to it!"

Kelli smiled back. "Well, I'm in the mood for a hot and dirty martini. You know, the one with the bleu-cheese-stuffed olives?"

Nina giggled. "Good girl! I'll be right back…"

Minutes later, each woman had a drink in her hand. Sipping her martini, Kelli took time to take in the bar. It was chic and modern, with clean angles and dark wood accents. The lighting was just low enough to create great ambience, and there were lots of little nooks and alcoves with dark, velvet-lined booths. As Kelli admired her surroundings, she completely tuned out, unaware that Nina was describing her latest relationship in great detail.

"Kelli? God, Kells, are you listening to a word I say? So, what do you think I should do, anyway?"

"Um, I guess you should do whatever you feel is right." Kelli had no idea to what Nina was referring. Her comment worked though, because Nina then launched into another detailed analysis of "he said, she said."

The bar was rapidly filling up with beautiful people. It was mostly an older, professional crowd, but Kelli noticed a few young twentysomethings in the mix. Their fresh faces made her feel self-conscious for just a moment, but she mentally shook it off. She felt good, sexy. And judging by the glances she was getting from a variety of male patrons, she could hold her own against a nubile twenty-three-year-old anytime.

There was one man in particular who kept glancing her way. He was across the room, leaning against the bar. He was perusing the room with his eyes as a four-star general might peruse a battlefield. Kelli gauged that he was about 5'10". Her eye was generally drawn to taller men, but there was something about this guy. He looked vaguely familiar—something about his eyes, but she couldn't figure out why. Maybe she had encountered him at a work function somewhere. *That must be it.*

She took in his physique, dressed in a tailored suit jacket over a simple black t-shirt and dark jeans with nice leather boots. His features were unusually striking. He was clean cut, with salt-and-pepper hair, olive skin, and a well-muscled frame. Their eyes met; she immediately noticed that his were a vivid green and warmly inviting. Kelli was becoming more and more conscious of him and was finding it even harder to pay attention to what Nina was saying.

Nina finally caught on and leaned forward to whisper, "Kelli, I think that guy over there is super into you! He keeps staring."

"Yeah, I've noticed. What do you think? I think he's really attractive. Do you think it's weird that he keeps looking at me like that?"

"Hell, no! He just wants to eat you up, that's all! Want me to call him over for you?"

"No, no. Don't do that. Maybe I'll just take this opportunity to get some drink refills."

"Sounds good, girl. Do it! In the meantime, there is a smoking hot guy at that corner table who has caught my eye...I might have to go say hello while you check out Mr. Intense over there."

Kelli decided to go to the ladies room first, to prepare herself before making her approach to the bar. She felt oddly nervous, with butterflies in her stomach. It had been so long since she had done anything like this. Did she even remember how to flirt, really flirt, and mean it? She reapplied her eyeliner and carefully smudged it along her upper eyelids, patted some powder lightly over her nose and cheeks from her purse compact, and topped things off with some more red lipstick. *Too much?* she wondered. But the mirror told her otherwise; she looked smoldering and intense, just as intense as the mystery man at the bar. She was ready.

Kelli walked out to the bar with confidence, and slid onto a bar stool a few seats down from the handsome stranger. She felt his eyes on her, like a brand burning into her neck. It was not an unpleasant sensation, but just the opposite. She ordered another hot and dirty martini; smiled coyly at the cute, young, male bartender; and then toyed with a cocktail napkin.

She felt him move next to her before she even saw him. There was indescribable warmth and the air tingled. She could smell the scent of his cologne: light, warm, and masculine. She glanced up and there he was, just inches away, softly smiling, almost grinning at her.

"Nice necklace. What's your name?"

Kelli unconsciously fingered her square, white gold and sapphire pendant. "Uh, thank you!" She was too flustered by his closeness to register his question about her name.

He looked at her intently and spoke again. His voice was rich and low. "I must say...you are an exceptionally beautiful, sexy woman."

Kelli was instantly mesmerized. His words, and his closeness, had a very strong effect on her. She suddenly felt like she'd had four or five drinks rather than two.

"That's very kind of you to say. Thank you."

"Ah, and you can take a compliment well. I like a confident, secure woman. It's a good sign."

"Sign of what?" Kelli asked, coyly.

He chuckled. "Assertiveness. Sexuality. I'm sure you're quite confident and uninhibited in bed. I can tell from a mile off."

With that, he leaned on the bar and signaled to the bartender. "I'd like a Henny on the rocks, please."

Kelli smiled, and toyed with the straw in her drink. She felt mildly tongue-tied. She found herself checking out the ring finger of his left hand. Nothing. Not even a tan line. She glanced up at him and noticed that he was looking closely at her left hand, which was still holding her drink. She suddenly felt self-conscious about the fact that she was still wearing her own wedding ring. *Why hadn't she taken it off?* She shifted her martini to her right hand and moved her left hand out of sight.

It was almost as if the stranger noticed or read her mind. He said, "Funny, isn't it? All of us here in this bar, looking for something that we don't have. Are you here looking for something, you with your long legs and beautiful hair?"

"Ha ha. Well, um, yeah, I guess you could say that. Sure. Yes. I'm looking for something."

"And what might that be? Let me guess…you are looking for a man who knows what he wants. *Really* knows what he wants." He smiled confidently at her and moved a little closer. She felt a thrill run up and down her spine in response. There was something about him that made her quiver. She wanted more.

Kelli looked into his strikingly green eyes and couldn't help noticing how beautiful his eyelashes were. She couldn't remember ever seeing such long lashes on a man. His face overall was intensely masculine; it was an exhilarating combination.

She took a deep breath. *Why not just be honest?* "Well, I'm making some big changes in my life; that's all."

His eyebrows shot up. "Oh? In what area?"

"Honestly? I've just been really unhappy for a long time, and I've had enough unhappiness. I want to start really living."

"Ah, I see. Let me guess…a bad marriage?"

Kelli suddenly felt vulnerable and exposed. She looked down and nodded.

"Well, I can certainly relate. I know all about that." His tone was unexpectedly sympathetic.

Her head shot back up and she looked at him in surprise. "Really? You were in a bad marriage?" It came as a shock to her that this handsome, charming man would have experienced anything similar to what she had with Paul.

It was his turn to look down at the floor. "Not was. I am."

"Wow. OK. If you don't mind me asking, what is your situation?"

"Oh, the usual. Married young…far too young. We have a lot in common in some areas but sooner rather than later, the sexual connection died. Completely. It's gone for good at this point."

"Ah. Yes. That happens." There was a pause. Kelli sensed that this was a turning point. She could steer the conversation in a different direction, out of dangerously personal waters, but part of her didn't want to. She wanted to hear more.

"And then? What now?"

He grimaced slightly. "A person can only take so much, and eventually I made some changes. I had some affairs. That's when it started, of course."

"Started? When what started?"

He looked at her intently. "You know, it's not often that you meet someone in a bar and start spilling your life history in five minutes. Particularly when that person is an exceptionally beautiful woman. On the other hand, I have to say, something about you inspires trust."

Kelli chuckled. "Well, as it happens, I listen to people for a living, so I guess that makes sense."

"Oh? Therapist?"

She nodded.

"What kind?"

"Um, actually, I'm a sex therapist."

Most people either looked delighted or terrified when Kelli told them her occupation. This man showed neither reaction. He simply looked intensely interested. Then he began to laugh softly. His laughter was melodic, and somehow soothing.

"Is that funny, somehow?"

"Oh, not really. I don't mean to laugh. It's just that it ties in so well with what I was about to tell you!"

Kelli looked at him quizzically. "How's that, then? Why?"

"Oh, I'll tell you in a minute. In the meantime, you need another drink."

Before Kelli could protest, he had signaled to the bartender. "Another hot and dirty martini, please."

Kelli was amazed and impressed that he had known what she was drinking.

"Wait…how did you…?"

He playfully took his finger and laid it ever so lightly against her lips. "Shhh. Never mind. Just accept it."

She was mesmerized. "Uh….OK. I will. So…you were about to tell me what was so funny about my job!"

"Well, like I said, it's not that it's funny. But let's just say…I am currently kind of compensating for the lack of sexual intimacy earlier in my marriage. It's just ironic that I would meet someone who specializes in that area. That's all."

"Ah. So…from what you're implying, it sounds like you're currently making up for lost time."

"Right. And things have gotten a little bit…um…let's just say, a little bit wild. Even out of control."

"I see. Out of control how, exactly?"

"The therapist in you is really coming out, huh? Or are you just getting excited?" His eyes twinkled and he leaned in a little closer. Kelli felt embarrassed, but aroused at the same time.

"I'm really sorry. I didn't mean to sound like I was grilling you. Never mind. It's really none of my business."

"No, no. It's fine actually. I was just teasing. I'm enjoying this. I don't mind talking about it."

"OK." She took another sip of her martini.

"So, basically, after my marriage, I really began to experiment, a lot, with a number of different women and different situations. Some of those situations were quite...alternative."

"Hmmm. Sounds interesting."

"Oh, it was. Is, I should say. I'm still in it, really. Maybe more than I should be."

"More than you should be? You aren't comfortable with it?"

He paused for a moment before responding. "It's not that I'm not comfortable. I'm very comfortable. Probably too comfortable. In fact, I think it's very interesting that I would meet you tonight, because recently I had even been considering therapy."

"Seriously? As in...sex therapy?"

"Yes, sex therapy. Like I said, it's odd that I would be thinking about it and then meet a real, live sex therapist. A sexy sex therapist, too." He winked and grinned at her.

Kelli felt a rush of conflicting emotions. What had seemed like an exciting sexual prospect was rapidly evolving into something entirely different: a client.

"So, tell me more about why you feel that you might need sex therapy," she probed.

He sighed. "Frankly, it's reaching a sort of saturation point. The sex is so...so compelling. For a while it was just an addiction. I couldn't get enough. Women, couples...alternative scenes, everything. I was experimenting all the time. But then the addiction took, I'm not sure how to say it exactly, a darker turn. It stopped being satisfying. I started wanting more. More from myself, more from my partners. Does that make sense?"

Kelli nodded. "Yes, of course it does. That's the natural progression, really."

"Well, and then some stuff happened..." He trailed off, and something in his tone made Kelli look more closely. A strange look, almost like pain, crossed over his chiseled features. "I don't want to talk about that now or here, though," he said. "Maybe we should save it for your office."

"My office?"

"Sure! Could I book an appointment with you? I'm not sure what it is exactly, but I feel like I'd really be able to trust you."

She felt a rush, like butterflies in her stomach. *Was this magnetic man really going to come to her as a client?* As soon as the thought crossed her mind, she remembered the rules of conduct for therapy. Taking him as a client would mean that she couldn't get involved with him. Ever. The thought turned her cold. *Do I really want to do that?*

On the other hand, the nurturing, caring part of her could sense that something was going on deep inside him. For all of his smooth facade, there was some pain buried there. She couldn't just let that go without doing anything about it, could she?

She let out a chuckle, almost ruefully. "Absolutely. Let me just grab a business card." She drew one out of her purse and handed it to him.

He examined the card and smiled. "All this time we've been chatting, and you hadn't told me your name. Kelli. Kelli Lemberg. It's very nice to meet you, Kelli." He reached out his hand and Kelli noticed how large it was, and how long his fingers were. "I'm Jake, by the way. Jake Furie Lapin."

Kelli took Jake's hand and it was like a lightning bolt hit her. The sexual electricity that coursed through their fingers and up her arm was unmistakable. *What have I done?* she wondered. *I can't believe I just agreed to take him as a client.*

To cover up her inner confusion, she commented, "You have an interesting name. I've been wondering this whole time…what is your ethnic background?"

He chuckled his throaty laugh.

"Oh, the typical American mutt. Born in Jersey City but part Greek, Dutch, German…maybe a few other nationalities thrown in there. What about you, Kelli Lemberg? I've told you my bad marriage story…now what's yours?"

Kelli felt much more interested in hearing more about Jake than she did in talking about Paul and her marriage, but she briefly outlined her situation. Jake listened attentively, nodding and occasionally asking a question. When Kelli finished, she noticed Jake glancing at her watch. She snuck a peek and was shocked to see that over an hour had passed since she had first approached the bar.

"Oh, I'm so sorry, but I really should go check on my friend Nina…but first we should set a date and time for your first session."

Jake leaned in closer, and she could smell the scent of him. It made her feel dizzy. "We will, but I do need to tell you about one thing, though," he said in a low voice. He was looking directly into her eyes, his gaze incredibly intense. "I can tell you more about the reasons for this when we are in session and get to know each other better, but I have a requirement…something I need in therapy."

Kelli had no idea what he could be talking about, but the smell of his skin and cologne was intoxicating. "OK. What is it?"

"For our first session, I need you to wear something for me."

"Wear something for you?" She drew back ever so slightly.

"Don't worry, don't worry. It's not what you think. But in order for me to feel comfortable with you, I need you to be dressed in a certain way."

"OK. What is it?"

"You need to wear a skirt and a button-up blouse." His tone was firm, and direct.

That doesn't seem too outrageous. "I can do that. Any particular kind?"

He nodded, not breaking his gaze. "Yes. The skirt must be black. Quite short. Above the knee. The blouse should be white. Thin material. The buttons should extend all the way from the neck to the waist."

He paused, and his expression was serious. "These details are extremely important if I am to feel comfortable with you. I won't be able to relax or to be vulnerable if my directions are not followed."

Kelli felt entranced, but the professional part of her did not find his request to be terribly odd. She had done stranger things than this for clients. There had been the woman who could only have sessions if Kelli wore a Phantom of the Opera mask and the young man in his twenties who insisted on bringing over fifty teddy bears and arranging them elaborately around her office. This was no different. She could do it. She also felt a secret thrill of pleasure running into her innermost places at the idea of wearing a short skirt and thin blouse for this man. Client or not, Jake was potently attractive, and her body reacted strongly to this fact, even while her mind struggled to remain detached.

Kelli suggested that they meet the next day, Friday. However, Jake told her that he needed to be at a charity event on Friday night, and that he would be leaving for Las Vegas for the weekend. Kelli wondered what he could be doing in Sin City, but was feeling too shy to press further, so they arranged to meet on the following Monday, at 4:00 p.m. Jake offered her his business card, and she toyed with it, before finally placing it on the bar.

A short time later, Nina came careening over to both of them and grabbed Kelli's arm. Her words slightly slurred, "Kell, let's get out of here. That creep in the corner won't leave me alone, and the hottie I was trying to seduce seems to have vanished into the toilet with some young guy. I'm over it. And…I'm just a little tipsy." Nina's eyes were faintly glazed, but she suddenly locked onto Jake. "Ooooh, well hello there, handsome! Where have YOU been all night?" Her eyes fell onto the business card on the counter. "Mmmm. Jake. Is that your name, big boy?"

Nina leaned forward and whispered, "Do you want to fuck me tonight, big boy? Because if you do, I'm yours…" but Jake pretended that he hadn't heard her.

Moving away from Nina, Jake smiled politely and responded, "Yes, Jake is my name. And I've been here, talking to your beautiful friend. But I'm afraid it's time for me to go now, also."

He turned and took Kelli's hand. "I'm very much looking forward to Monday," he said in a low voice. He raised her hand to his lips and brushed it ever so lightly. "Thank you." His eyes were intensely green, but as he turned, they almost looked deep blue. It was startling, and had a thrilling effect. Kelli's stomach lurched.

He turned, but before Kelli could quite recover from the sensation of his lips on her skin, he was gone.

"God, Kelli. Who IS he? You've struck gold there." Nina picked up the business card and stared at it intently before handing it to Kelli.

"Hmmm. Yeah, well, he's going to be a client of mine, so I can't really think that way. But in any case, it is weird, because he seems so familiar to me. I feel like I have definitely met him somewhere before, but I can't put my finger on it," Kelli mused.

Nina shrugged. "Someone that hot... Oh, you'd remember. You probably just saw him in your dreams!" She giggled, and then paused. "You know, now that you mention it...I feel like he seemed familiar to me, too. Do you think he's famous? Maybe he's a reality TV star or B-list celeb and we just can't place it."

Kelli thought for a moment. "I don't know. Maybe. It's so odd, though. I can't figure it out."

"Well, you're the one who is going to have him sitting in your office. My god! I know exactly what I would do if I got him alone," Nina said, as she made a lewd slurping noise.

Kelli hardly noticed Nina's coarse joke. She was transfixed, staring at the door where she'd seen Jake exit the building. The whole room felt empty without him. Suddenly, she realized something, and started to laugh softly. The whole time she had been talking to Jake, she hadn't thought of her online mishaps. Not even once. Jake's charm and attentiveness had pushed the thought right out of her mind.

"What's so funny, Kelli? Why the hell are you laughing?" Nina slurred.

"Oh, nothing. Nothing at all. Come on. Let's get you home."

{ 3 }

Monday. Monday. Monday. It was a mantra echoing through her brain. Seeing Jake again was all that Kelli could think about. The few days that passed between meeting Jake on Thursday night and his therapy appointment on Monday afternoon seemed like an eternity. Kelli found herself adding up the hours and moments until their first session. *What was it about him?* There was something so mysterious and appealing. She kept reminding herself that therapists weren't allowed to get involved with clients, but time and time again, she found herself replaying the events in the bar, over and over again. Kelli re-ran each and every detail of their conversation, trying to find clues as to who he was and what their interaction on Monday might be like. She was incredibly excited, but was trying not to admit it to herself.

Nina wasn't much help, either. "My GOD," she said over lunch the next day, "I cannot believe the chemistry that was there between the two of you. You do realize that it was completely electric, right? I kept thinking that the bar was going to burst into flames. Do you seriously think that you are going to be able to keep him as a client without jumping him?" She nibbled on the very tip of a breadstick, suggestively, and looked at Kelli, while batting her eyelashes.

Kelli had wondered the same thing herself several times, but she acted mildly offended. "Nina! What do you think I am? Yes, of course I can take him as a client. I'm a professional. This is what I do. I can separate my own personal feelings from my work." Inside, she was anything but certain of this fact. She couldn't stop thinking of him, after all.

She obviously didn't sound convincing. Nina wrinkled up her nose slightly. "Hmmmm. Well, whatever. I give it two months, tops, before you're banging him." Her friend grinned wickedly and popped a cherry tomato into her mouth. Kelli just rolled her eyes and ignored her, but felt the familiar pang of butterflies inside her stomach.

When it finally rolled around, Monday morning itself was the worst. Kelli had a day packed full of clients, and could barely focus on what they were saying to her. She sat through some of her regulars, listening half-heartedly to freckle-faced Sarah droning on about her latest one-night stand and how it related to her parents' relationship, and then to crazy-eyed Vincent's dissection of his ongoing obsession with his boss. Part of her felt guilty that she was not giving her full attention to her patients, but another part of her felt exactly like a teenage girl going to the prom. She wasn't really admitting it fully, but the fact of the matter was that she simply could not wait to see Jake again.

In preparation for her session with him, she had dressed in the exact clothes that he had specified: a short black skirt and thin, white muslin blouse with buttons from her chin to her waist. She felt a thrill of anticipation at the idea of him being pleased and satisfied with her outfit. "It's for his therapy," she told herself, "All for his therapy."

At 3:50 p.m., her last client left, and Kelli felt completely frazzled. An iced vanilla chai…now that was just the thing to calm her down and make her feel a little better before Jake arrived. She let her secretary know where she was headed and walked briskly down to her favorite street-side coffee stand.

Unfortunately, there was a line at the stand, and by the time Kelli had her drink it was already 4 p.m. *He's probably there right now,* she thought, *waiting for me.* The thought made her stomach twist into knots, and she felt almost nauseous. She walked back as briskly as she could without breaking a sweat, and came into the office ten minutes late.

"Your four o'clock is here and waiting in the therapy room," her secretary told her, sounding bored.

Kelli suddenly realized that she was sweating a little. "Let him know that I'll be right in," she instructed, and went straight to the ladies room. She got out her compact and dabbed on a little face powder along with some nude lipstick and brown eye shadow. The makeup made her feel much better, more secure, armored.

She stepped back into the foyer. *Here we go*, Kelli thought, as she opened the door.

The afternoon light was fading and it took Kelli a moment for her eyes to adjust to the dimness of the room. When they did, she was slightly shocked to realize that Jake was not sitting in any of the usual spots that clients generally chose. Instead, he was in the dead center of the room, in Kelli's usual therapist's chair, gazing directly at her as she entered. One of his ankles was resting on his other knee, and his arms were open and spread out across the back of the chair. The therapist in Kelli recognized his body language and posture immediately. *Confident. Assertive. Secure.*

She took in the rest of his appearance. He looked noticeably tanner, and she thought of what he had told her about going to Vegas. She couldn't help but imagine him on the Strip, sipping a drink in the lounge of one of the higher-end casinos, and she felt a twinge of desire at the thought. She also noticed he was wearing a gray, pin-striped suit that was obviously from a top designer; she suspected it was Armani. Even from the doorway, she could tell that the material was heavy and of the highest quality. His shirt was a crisp white and looked like a silk/cotton blend. It was impeccably ironed, and the cuffs of the shirt were pinned with solid, square-shaped cuff links with an embossed pattern on them. The patina of the cuff links was that of a dull, antique silver. His tie was also obviously designer and a deep, brick red color that complemented the suit and conveyed a strong sense of power and control. His shoes were expensive black leather, and were void of any scratches or scuffs.

Before she could open her mouth, he spoke. "You're late, Kelli." The tone of his voice was calm but had an undertone of steel.

Kelli was instantly flustered and apologetic. "Oh, yes, I'm sorry about…"

Before she could finish her sentence, Jake was out of the chair and standing in front of her. He reached out and silenced her with a finger across her lips. "Shhhhh."

His finger pressed hard against her lips produced an immediately sexual effect on Kelli. She felt a jolt of electricity running from his hand down her body and between her legs. She could tell that she had just become instantly wet as she stared motionlessly into his green eyes.

He spoke her name again. "Kelli, you were late. That is not acceptable. You must, and I repeat, *must* be on time for our sessions. With no exceptions." He paused, and as he did so, he removed his red tie from around his neck with nimble fingers. Kelli remained wordless.

Jake held up his tie, folding it over itself, and continued, "If you are late again, there will be consequences. I will need to administer discipline to you. Do you understand what I'm saying?"

Kelli wasn't sure if she understood him correctly or not, but what she was sure of was that her nipples were completely hard through the thin fabric of her shirt, so hard that they actually hurt. She nodded back to him mutely.

"I need words from you, Kelli," Jake said. "Answer me with a yes or a no."

"Y…yes," Kelli managed to whisper.

"Good girl. At the end of our session, I will tell you more about my discipline. But for now, we may begin. Take a seat."

Jake returned to the therapist's chair in the center of the room, leaving Kelli the choice of several other seats that were arranged in a semicircle. She sank into the nearest armchair feeling grateful to be off her feet. The tension between them was so palpable that she felt like she might pass out if she kept standing. This dynamic was like no other she had ever experienced. It was clear that Jake had taken control of the situation and his mastery was intoxicating to her. She knew, without even checking, that her G-string was soaked through with her arousal. Just his touch and his firm tone had been enough to produce that physical effect. If this is how the session was starting, she wasn't sure how she was going to make it all the way through.

He was gazing at her silently, and with a start, she realized that he was waiting for her to speak. Kelli suddenly noticed that when he removed his tie, he had also undone the top couple of buttons on his shirt, giving the slightest hint beneath of a smooth and chiseled chest. Kelli was incredibly turned on by the thought of seeing him shirtless and quickly spoke as a way to hide her instinctual lust and confusion.

"Uh, so, I guess…why don't we start with you telling me about your weekend? You were going to be quite busy, I remember. What about the charity event? How was it?"

Jake spoke. "The charity event was great. I guess I should start from the beginning and fill you in on how I came to be there. I received an invite from an upscale burger joint that was hosting a charity event in another county. I decided to attend and when I arrived at the place, it was extremely busy; packed, in fact. The charity event had already begun. It was my first visit to this particular restaurant and I was excited to try their cuisine. When I sat down, I ordered a tuna appetizer and one of their craft beers. Next to me was a couple. He was pretty nondescript, just your average guy. Nothing special. In fact, I noticed that he was wearing jeans that were pretty sloppy, given the nature of the event. His date even seemed a little bit embarrassed to be with him. She was very pretty. Slim, dark hair, and a great set of tits. She was sitting down, so I couldn't see her ass, but my imagination was already going crazy."

Kelli smiled. "An ass guy, huh?"

Jake grinned back. "Oh yeah. Ass and legs, all the way. In any case, I happened to notice that the couple had a very unusual clam appetizer. Because food is one of my great loves, I checked it out and stared at it for quite a while. This caught the attention of the brunette, who kept glancing over at me and smiling. Our eyes met at several points, and I could tell that she found me attractive. As the night continued, I had another one of the craft beers, which put me in a great mood.

"My appetizer arrived, and the brunette leaned over and asked, 'What is that?' I had only eaten half of it because I wasn't enjoying it, but I told her, 'It's a peppered tuna appetizer, which I normally order in my favorite sushi restaurant. This one really isn't doing it for me. In fact, the tuna seems a bit rotten.'

"She was appalled. 'That's not OK. Are you going to complain?' I shrugged. 'Hey, I'm here to support the charity, not to make trouble over the food. If I want great sushi, there are plenty of other places I can go.'

"She sparked a new part of the conversation when she asked me about my favorite sushi restaurant, and we started talking about sushi restaurants in general. She mentioned another one close by that was for a high-end crowd, and I told her I had been there a few times. Then I informed her of a place where I go to that is a bit more low key, but was probably the best sushi in New Jersey. 'Maybe one day I will take you there.' I threw the line out at her to see if she would bite."

Kelli interrupted, "Wait, wasn't she with someone?"

"Yes, she was. In fact, I felt a little awkward because the guy I thought was her date was joining in our conversation back and forth. He seemed to cut out sometimes and put himself away from the conversation, so I thought it could have been her brother or perhaps a coworker. I wasn't really sure what to make of the guy with her. I really had no intention of meeting or flirting with anybody. I was just going there to support a charity.

"As the night wore on, I found out that her name was Megan, and at one point she even offered to share her appetizer. 'Would you like to have some of my clam?' she asked with a flirtatious smile.

"'I prefer my clams to be totally raw and smooth.'

"She smiled and said, 'Well mine has a small carpet on it. Would that be okay?'

"'In my lifestyle, I prefer to have it smooth and bare. I might have to take it off for you,' I dared.

"She looked at me curiously, and then asked, 'What is your lifestyle?'

"'I am into the BDSM lifestyle,' I answered her.

"Megan said, 'Oh wow. I've heard of that. I'm very curious about it, but I don't know what to do, or how to go about exploring the BDSM lifestyle.'

"'There is plenty of reading to do, and you should definitely research it first before getting into the lifestyle,' I informed her.

"We started to talk a little bit further when her date left to use the bathroom. 'Would you be willing to show me?' she probed.

"I smiled at her. 'Hmm. We will just have to see.'

"Changing the subject, she asked, 'What do you do?'

"'I work in banking.' I didn't give her a clue that I am working on an erotica novel, as that typically scares women away.

"She noticed the scar on my arm and I told her that it came from a childhood tragedy on a subway, and that I didn't even notice it anymore. She put her nails on the scar and glided her hand lightly across it. 'Does it hurt?' she inquired.

"'Not at all,' I replied.

"Megan proceeded to tell me that she had scars of her own. I asked her what they were from, and she proceeded to tell me a little bit about her past and that she was in an abusive relationship a few years ago. She was in it for quite a long time; the partner had actually stabbed her a couple of times in the stomach and once in the ribs. The stab wounds didn't go deep, but they were enough to leave scars on her body that she was self-conscious about. She shared some of her fears and insecurities with me. 'I'm afraid no one will find me attractive anymore,' she said.

"'The right man will come into your life. Don't worry about your scars. Be confident in who you are,' I told her.

"She got quiet for a moment and then she asked, 'What exactly do you do in banking?'

"I replied, 'I'm in the mortgage division of the bank. I help clients finance homes that they might want to refinance or purchase.'

"She told me she was considering buying a home in the area and that she may need my help one day. I still felt awkward because the person she had come with had long since returned from the bathroom and was sitting with her once again. I felt some uneasiness coming from him. It wasn't really my style to come between a female and her date.

"'Here is my card. If you need any help you can give me a call,' I said while handing both her and her date cards so that I could assure him that I wasn't going after his date.

"No sooner had I paid my tab and left, she sent me a text. She excused herself for texting me without giving me her number first at the bar. The essence of Megan's text was that she had a really good time talking to me at the bar and wanted to know if I cared to meet her for extra drinks at another place to continue the conversation.

"I answered, 'You know what? I am living life to the fullest at this point. Why not? It's still a little early, only 11:30 p.m. at night. Let's continue the conversation and go for more drinks. Where would you like to go?'

"'How about my place?' was Megan's response, as she gave me her address.

Kelli commented, "Wow, that's bold. Do you always have that effect on women, where they just throw themselves at you?"

Jake shrugged. "I suppose. Women like a man who is confident and knows what he wants."

"So what happened next?" asked Kelli.

"When I got her text, I chuckled of course and texted back, 'Well, isn't your friend with you?'

"'Oh him, that was a blind date. It went sour from the moment we met. He wasn't into me at all and only talked about himself. I like the fact that you asked questions about me, listened to my responses, and told me more about yourself. I really enjoyed the time with you. I live in a gated community. I will buzz you in,' she texted back.

"At this point, I should add that Megan and I had an earlier discussion about food while at the charity event. I informed her that I enjoyed cooking and experimenting with certain dishes. I read a lot about cooking, dieting, and health, and so did she. She lived in a townhouse, and due to the layout we had to go through her kitchen to get to her non-formal living area. I noticed she had some expensive cooking utensils on the counter and complimented her on them. She made us some drinks as we were talking, and I told her that I enjoy cranberry vodka after a couple of beers, so she made one for the each of us.

"After a few drinks, she got closer to me and lunged in quickly for a kiss. Once we started kissing a bit she said to me, 'I know you are into the BDSM lifestyle. I want you to teach me. Tell me what it's about and train me to become a submissive.'

"'I would be willing to train you, but I do not have time for a full-blown relationship,' I responded.

"'I understand. Right now I want to take things slow. I am trying to start my life over after my abusive relationship,' she stated.

"We made our way to the bedroom, and I noticed she had a nice candle layout. We got naked quickly. 'Do you have any belts and thin sheets?' I asked.

"She showed me where she kept them and I grabbed a couple of her belts and sheets. 'Do you trust me?' I asked her.

"'The moment I started talking to you, I loved your voice. I trust you 1,000%,' she replied.

"I took the two sheets and bound her legs wide open to the posts and took a few of her belts and tied her wrists to the headboard. She seemed very nervous at first. 'Relax,' I said to her, 'Everything will be fine.'

"'Don't worry. Do what you want to do to me,' she answered, probably somewhat due to her intoxicated state, but it set things at ease.

"I lit about six or seven of her candles. 'These are going to come into play at some point in the night,' I informed her. She looked a bit confused.

"'This has to come off,' I said, referring to the thin strip of hair above her clam.

"'That's fine,' she assured me, 'I promise to shave it off tomorrow or tonight after we have sex.'

"'No,' I said, 'I'm going to take care of it right now.' I went to the bathroom and took out her cream and razor while she was bound to the bed. I carefully shaved the excess hair that was above her clam. At that point, I could tell that she trusted me 1,000% because I did a great job of cleaning her up.

"'Next time, make sure you are smooth and ready for me,' I demanded.

"'I will,' she said.

"'No. Say, "Yes, Sir,"' I commanded. She understood and promptly nodded her head and bit her tongue.

"The candles had been lit awhile, so I grabbed one and dripped some wax on her nipples, legs, and clit. She flinched a few times, but quickly realized that she enjoyed the pain and pleasure, just as I had learned when I lost my virginity. I didn't drip any wax on her scars, but instead I kissed all of her scars. 'You are a beautiful woman. Don't ever let a man bring you down in that way,' I told her. She almost teared up in happiness.

"All the wax had dried in drops on her legs. 'I will be right back,' I assured her. I went into her beautiful gourmet kitchen and found a filet knife for cutting fish. When I returned to the bedroom, she had a horrified look on her face.

"'Don't worry,' I said while calming her.

"I then slowly and carefully peeled all of the wax off of her body. She was quivering and panting, most likely reliving the terror of her abusive past. After I removed all of the wax, I returned the knife to the kitchen, reentered the bedroom, and immediately released her from her bindings. As soon as she was free, she lunged and grabbed me. 'Thank you so much! I'm very much in love with you!' she said excitedly.

"'You are not in love with me at this point. Just now, you learned what BDSM is all about. It's about trust and being open with one another,' I said to her. 'We are not going to have sex tonight, but instead, we are going to rest and absorb what we have gone through. We will have sex in the morning.'

"The next morning when I woke up next to her, I found myself to be extremely hard. Without saying a word, I spooned her from behind and began to play with her nipples. I discovered she had extremely sensitive nipples, and she started moaning and grinding against me. After running my hands up and down her body for a while and kissing her neck, I flipped her over with her legs over my shoulders. I massaged her pussy firmly for a while and then slid two fingers inside; she was soaking wet. Her pussy juices were flowing and I couldn't wait to taste them. I went down on her slowly, and flicked her clit with my tongue.

"I started slowly kissing all around her juicy lips, and began to pick up the pace when I noticed her breathing got very hard and fast. 'I need you inside me,' she whispered.

"Without saying a word, I entered her and pushed all the way inside. She moaned loudly and clenched around me. I fucked her slowly, letting her savor every inch, before upping the intensity. She was close to cumming already and started to moan louder. While still inside her and thrusting, I leaned down and kissed her passionately, first on the mouth and then all over her neck and chest. I fingered her nipple with one hand and braced myself with the other as I went deeper and deeper insider of her.

"She was practically shrieking by this point, and I knew she was going to cum hard. Sure enough, just a few seconds later her whole body bucked and I felt her spasms around my cock. With one final thrust, I came hard with her. It was incredible, and I knew she wouldn't forget it. I wanted to give her a lesson in trusting a man, and showing her the type of man she should be with."

"Wow," said Kelli. "That's amazing. What happened next?"

"Well," Jake replied. "It was now 7:15 a.m. In spite of the great sex we'd just had, I'd been restless all night and something just wasn't sitting right inside me. Megan lay peacefully on my chest, holding me securely, comfortingly. I wanted to do something special for her, make her breakfast, and make her cum hard again in our next sex session. I slid my way out of the bed and gracefully made my way to the kitchen. *Omelet or Pancakes*, I thought. The answer came right away: pancakes with berries. We would need the energy to burn off our upcoming intense sex session.

"I started to prepare the mix, thinking to myself, *It should only take twenty minutes to make a few nice stacks.* I wanted this to be perfect. Thankfully, she had fresh strawberries and blueberries in the fridge, and a healthy multigrain pancake mix in her pantry. *Organic maple syrup.* Awesome, I thought. As I started to prepare the meal, I heard a noise and looked over to spot her phone, just sitting there on the kitchen counter. I was curious. *Who is this girl, really?* I wondered.

"I picked up the phone and saw that it was lit up from a text message. I suppose that most men wouldn't have intruded, but then…I'm not most men. So I opened the text and read the contents. It was from a guy and it read: 'Megan, I'm sorry about last night. I won't bring up our past again, can I bring over a few movies tonight and snuggle like we used to?' Next to the message there was an image she had attached to the contact details and the name of the sender. Mark: her date from the bar last night.

"*Fuck!* I thought. *Hmmmm.* Maybe she wasn't as unattached as she had led me to believe. Without a second thought, I replied back for her, "Mark, you know what, come over now. Be here no sooner than 8:00 a.m., I'm making breakfast, let's talk."

":-) was the response back.

"I put the phone down, turned around, and Megan was standing in the doorway. She was dressed in only my white button-down shirt, as she made her way into the kitchen, stretching sexily.

"'Jake, last night was amazing; I can't wait to feel you inside me again. Fuck, you're good!' I stared at her, this time with distrust. I didn't want to let her know what I was thinking, though, so I pretended that everything was fine.

"'Babe, sit down. I'm making breakfast.' I furiously finished the mix, poured several pancakes into the pan, and chopped up the berries as the pancakes were cooking. Quickly getting two plates, I made two healthy stacks with fruit and plain yogurt, and placed the berries on top. I looked over at her and could tell that she was quite impressed by my kitchen skills. However, my attention wasn't on the food anymore. I was glancing at the kitchen clock. It read 7:40 a.m. *Not much time.* I left both finished plates on the counter, made my way to the kitchen table, and sat down across from her.

"'Megan, we need to have a lesson. Come here.' She grinned at me, and I knew what she was thinking. She was remembering the sizzling hot vanilla sex that we had just an hour or so before. She was expecting more of the same, but didn't yet realize that this lesson wasn't going to be pleasant for her.

"She quickly left her chair and walked over to me. I firmly grabbed her long wavy hair and knotted it around my left fist, pulling her across my lap. Holding her down with her hair in my left hand, I started to firmly spank her ass with my right hand, hitting as hard as I could. I licked my right palm a few times to make it sting, I wanted to leave impressions on her ass.

"I finished and glanced at the clock again; it was 7:43 a.m.

"I threw her on top of the table, and while holding her arms down, I made my way to her thighs with my mouth. The spanking had shocked her somewhat, but she was still wet. When I flicked her fleshy button with my tongue, she moaned, 'Oh yes, please, Jake. I need this, take me.' I sucked on her thigh and bit down hard, leaving my mark on her inner thigh.

"The clock said 7:45 a.m. I pulled myself up and she grabbed my cock. I looked at her, and placed my hand firmly around her throat. She eagerly slid my cock inside her wet pussy.

"'Fuck me. Fuck me hard.' Still grabbing her throat, I pounded her furiously with fast, hard thrusts, harder than she had ever felt before. Her breasts were bouncing up and down and every thrust brought a new sound out of her lips. She was panting like an animal and shouting my name.

"'Jake! Oh my god, Jake! I am so close. Keep fucking me, right there, please fuck me harder!'

"Glancing at the clock, I saw it was 7:50 a.m. I kept fucking her until she was at the edge. Then, just before she came, I stopped. Completely.

"She was totally bewildered. 'Jake, what are you doing? I'm so close. Why are you stopping?'

"'Beautiful, it's 7:53 a.m., and your *BLIND* date, Mark, will be here soon to snuggle and watch movies like old times,' I said sarcastically.

"She bowed her head. She knew exactly what was happening: She had lied to me about her date.

"'Serve him breakfast and talk to him. Tell him the truth,' I told her firmly. 'When you are ready to be honest with me, call me and let me know. I have a flight out to Vegas this afternoon from Philadelphia airport, so you can call me when I am out there. BDSM is not a game. There is no room for lies or sidestepping issues. It's about being honest and trustworthy. If you lie to me now, how will I know you won't lie to me again so you can sleep with another guy? Understand?'

"She nodded her head in understanding.

"It was 7:55 a.m. I grabbed my belongings, and left her place feeling disgusted. Almost immediately, my phone lit up with a new message from her: 'I'm sorry. I want to be with you.' I didn't respond back; I needed to get home and get ready for my trip to Vegas."

"Impressive," said Kelli. "It's good to know that you can speak your mind so clearly and stick to your beliefs." Jake's story was making her feel warm all over. She couldn't believe how strong he was, and she felt moved by what he told her.

She pulled herself together and realized that he was gazing at her intently. He was waiting for her to say something.

"So, uh, that was what happened from the charity event. What about the trip to Vegas?"

"Well, driving home to pack for the trip, my phone kept alerting me of new messages from Megan. I wasn't responding but they just kept coming:

" *'I'm sorry'*

" *'Please talk to me'*

" *'Hello, Jake'*

" *'I need to talk to you, to explain'*

" *'Please don't hate me. I know what I did was wrong'*

" 'I need to talk to you'

" 'Don't hate me, please'

" 'Call me'

"All the messages were coming in about ten seconds apart. I just let them sit for a while. She needed to get worried and really think about what had taken place. I wasn't going to be another one of these guys that she could lie to.

"In between messages from Megan, I got a new text from an old friend. It was someone that I'd had a casual fling with in the past. I had actually wanted to go deeper with her, but it had remained casual.

"'Hi' was the message. My heart raced fiercely. Our paths had crossed several times, and I wasn't sure if I was ready for them to cross again after the last time. She had hurt me a lot. I thought it was over and buried by now, but obviously, it's never over. It's never finished business, always unfinished."

Kelli smiled again. "It's good to know that someone can get through to you," she said. "I see that you have a heart, after all."

Jake nodded and continued with his story.

"'Hey V, how r u?' I responded.

"'Talk? Are you alone?' she asked.

"'Kinda, getting ready to pack for Vegas, can I call you in a bit?'

"'KK,' she responded.

"I knew something had to be wrong. V had only ever texted me when she felt lonely or wanted to talk about something going on in her life.

"By this time, I was home and packing quickly for my short trip. Already the drama was rolling in.

"I thought about the events of the past twenty-four hours. I did like Megan, a lot. I felt bad about leaving her in such a state of despair and arousal, but I didn't appreciate being lied to or misled. *Maybe I should give her a second chance?*

"In the meantime, I had to figure out what do I do about my old friend. It occurred to me that I would have to open up to Megan a bit more, make sure she knew everything about me, and let her know that I cannot commit to any relationship right now.

"Finally, I sent her a text to explain myself and put her mind somewhat at ease.

"'Megan, I am upset, but I understand why you did what you did. I've been there before, afraid of the truth. I'll call you when I am at the gate, as I'll probably have thirty minutes or so to kill, OK?'

"'OMG, thank you Sir xo,' she replied.

"As I drove to the airport, I thought about the fact that V was texting me. It had to be something major; she usually only reached out to me when she was in significant pain. *What could it be?* I knew that she had recently been involved with a guy who I knew was a complete player. I had tried to warn V about him, and knew that she might get hurt, but she'd been obsessed with winning him over. I knew that it was really about the chase on both sides, and that it wouldn't last, but she was determined to pursue the relationship.

"I called her and within a few minutes, she had broken down in tears. He had left her, just like I had predicted. I gave her some words of comfort. It really bothered me to hear her in pain. I tried to give her the support that she needed, and she eventually calmed down. I told her that when I got back from my Vegas trip that we could get together and talk about things.

"After I checked in and got through security at the airport, I decided to give Megan a call. I figured that I would at least give her a chance to explain herself. She was incredibly grateful and told me over and over again how sorry she was for having deceived me. I told her that I liked her a lot but that I needed for us to be completely transparent with one another from this point forward. There could be no room for any lies.

"Megan immediately agreed, and I told her that I was going to be very busy on the Vegas trip, particularly as I was planning to participate in several poker tournaments. However, I also told her that I wanted to take her out for dinner when I came back from Vegas, so that we could get to know each other better."

Kelli felt approving. "Good for you!" she said. "I think second chances are important." She thought of how many times she had given Paul a second, third, and fourth chance. It had been the right thing to do at the time, even if those days were coming to an end.

"So, you still haven't told me about Vegas! What happened when you got there?"

"Well, I was ready for a swim, so I got my swim trunks on and headed for the pool. A bunch of my poker buddies were already there and having beers, so I joined them. What immediately caught my eye was the fact that all the guys were sitting in a row, and there was one empty chair. Next to the empty chair was an extraordinarily beautiful woman. Of course, I sat in the empty chair.

"I sat for a while making small talk with my buddies, but eventually the woman turned to me and struck up a conversation. She asked about the tournament and we got into a great conversation. I can always tell when a woman is interested or available, and this was definitely one of those situations. We started to talk more intimately, and she told me that her boyfriend was also in the pool bragging up his poker tournament prowess. She confessed to me that she traveled all over the country with him, but that she never actually got to spend time with him.

"'What do you mean?' I asked her.

"She replied, 'Well, it's just that he's always gambling, sleeping, or out drinking with his buddies! I hardly ever get to see him.'

"I leaned in and gazed into her eyes. 'Do you get lonely?'

"She nodded slowly. 'Yes. Yes I do. I just want to be able to spend quality time with the man I love.'

"We talked for a few minutes longer before she turned to me. 'Jake, I know this might be a lot to ask and you might be busy, but would you be able to just hang out with me for a while? Just dinner and talking?'

"I agreed. I was still thinking of both Megan and V, but it seemed like a little friendly company with a beautiful woman couldn't hurt.

"She stood up, and I admired her gorgeous, svelte figure as she told me that she was going to her room to get ready for dinner.

"After she left, a guy came out of the pool and approached me. It turned out that he was her boyfriend. He'd seen me talking to her and felt threatened, I suppose.

"He asked me what I'd talked about with her and I told him we'd just chatted about various things. Then he proceeded to tell me that he had met a different girl just hours before and planned to 'tap that' during the evening."

Kelli was horrified. "What? He actually TOLD you that?"

Jake nodded. "Yeah. The guy was that arrogant and that stupid. I couldn't believe that he had such a stunning girlfriend and would treat her like that. I decided right then and there that I was going to teach him a lesson, somehow."

Kelli nodded in agreement. "I don't blame you. So what happened next?"

Jake continued, "I asked the boyfriend what his plans were with this other girl. He told me that he was going to wine and dine this other woman before going to her hotel room to fuck her. Without giving him any hint of my motives, I asked which restaurant he was going to take her to, which he told me immediately. The guy was a pompous asshole who enjoyed bragging about his cheating habits. I had a plan in mind, though.

"I left the pool and headed up to my room to shower and change. On the way, I texted the beautiful girl, Rachelle, and told her to meet me at a famous restaurant inside one of the nicest casinos on the Strip. What I didn't tell her was that this was the same restaurant her boyfriend was going to, and around the same time.

"She agreed, and we met as planned. She looked even more beautiful, wearing a sexy metallic dress and heels. We went inside and as we were waiting for our table, we chatted. Just then I saw what I had been waiting for. Her boyfriend was across the room, holding hands and stroking his date. I didn't hesitate; I immediately told Rachelle to look. She gasped, and then she began to cry. She was crying hard, clearly distraught, and I didn't want her to be embarrassed by drawing attention to herself, so I cradled her head against my chest and rocked back and forth a little, comforting her.

"She eventually calmed down and looked up at me. 'How did you know?' she whispered.

"I kept holding her, and said in a soothing voice, 'I just did. I have a good grasp on human nature and I just knew he wasn't a good guy.'

"'What am I going to do?' Rachelle asked. She wiped her face and stared up at me with beautiful blue eyes.

"'I know exactly what you are going to do. You are going to get revenge. Your boyfriend was actually talking to me earlier. He told me that you are bisexual. Is that true?'

"She nodded. 'Yeah, it's true.'

"'Well, what he said was that sometimes after he cheats on you with another woman, he doesn't even bother to shower or clean up before coming home and fucking you. He figures that it doesn't matter much if you smell or taste another woman's juices.'

"Her face drained of color. She was starting to look furious. 'That fucking pig! I knew it! I fucking knew it!'

"'Yeah, well this is what you are going to do now. When he gets home tonight, don't even give him a chance to shower or whatever. Grab him, and go straight for a French kiss. Lots and lots of tongue. Then stop, and tell him very calmly that you saw him with the other girl at the restaurant. After that, proceed to tell him that you immediately hooked up with another man. You can pretend that it was me. Tell him that you let me penetrate every part of your body, and that you swallowed a huge load of my cum. We know it's not true, but tell him that anyway. Tell him that you didn't rinse or brush your teeth. Then ask him how he likes the idea of drinking down another man's juices.'

"She looked slightly horrified. 'That's... really gross,' she said.

"'Yeah, I know. And that's the point. You aren't really going to do that, but making him think that you did will teach him a lesson.'

"She seemed to take this in, and nodded.

"We enjoyed a pleasant dinner together, and then I told her that I needed to go back to my room to get ready for my flight out the next day.

"Early that morning, about 2:00 a.m., I got a text message from

Rachelle. 'OMG, Jake, thank u soooooo much!' it said. She had tried my plan and it had worked like a charm. He admitted to having cheated on her dozens of times and they broke up. She was sad, but relieved overall. She thanked me again and told me to stay in touch. 'If u ever need anything or just want to talk, please let me know!' she said. 'Can I give you a hug before you leave?'

"'Sure, I'm packed and just waiting for my cab. It arrives at 4:00 a.m., so I have some time to kill. I'll be up to your room in a few minutes.'

"I arrived at her room and knocked on the door. She immediately jumped out of the room, pulled me inside and gave me the biggest hug. Felt amazing. I held her tight, feeling the pain that she had just gone through. Almost immediately, she went to her knees and unbuttoned my ripped jeans.

"'Commando, mmmmmm. I need to taste you, Jake. I want to taste your juices. Please fuck my face; I want to take your full load inside my mouth.'

"I grabbed her hair and slowly guided her, having her stroke me up and down my shaft, feeling her throat and cheeks, alternating the speed, thrust, and position.

"'I don't cum easy babe, so let me do this for you. I don't have a ton of time,' I told her. I hit her mouth with the perfect spot of my cock, the only spot that makes me cum. Pulling her head backwards and fucking her sexy mouth deep, I was starting to get larger and thicker, and I watched as her eyes teared up a bit, anxious with excitement. I exploded hard, viciously inside her mouth, deep; all the juices poured down her throat. She anxiously continued to suck every drop from my cock.

"'Rachelle, you are amazing,' I sighed.

"She kept sucking, but more slowly this time, taking every drop, and finished. 'Jake, I will always be indebted to you, and YOU can fuck me ANYTIME. Just text me when you are in town or in LA.'

"I nodded, kissed her, and left. She really felt indebted and was serious about remaining friends forever."

"I can see why!" Kelli commented. "You stood up for her and helped her get out of an unhealthy relationship. That counts for a lot, you know." Again, she couldn't help but think of her own terrible marriage to Paul. If only she could break free, too. She stole a glance at Jake and wondered if he would ever be able to help her like he had helped Rachelle.

Jake smiled at her. "Crazy weekend, huh?" he chuckled. "I'm not going to pretend that they are all this eventful, but this one was pretty hectic. But I'm here now, with you."

He paused for a second, then continued, "I see that you are wearing what I asked you to wear. Good. Why don't you stand up and turn around so I can see it?"

As if under the influence of a drug, Kelli slowly rose, obediently and wordlessly, and turned in a slow circle. When she returned to her original position, she saw that Jake's eyes were smoldering appreciatively. She could hardly look away from him. She remained standing until he spoke again.

He set his folded tie on the table next to his chair and continued. "You may sit down now, Kelli. Now, what were you saying?"

She sat, caught her breath, and began again, struggling to keep what she hoped was a professional tone. "So, um, this is our first session, so, uh, you've filled me in on your weekend. Now, why don't you...why don't you tell me about what happened in your marriage? How did things start to go wrong?" As she heard the words come out of her mouth, she realized that she sounded meek, shaky, and uncertain like a little girl. Jake seemed to have that effect on her.

He, on the other hand, continued to be completely relaxed and in control. He waited for a moment or two and then began to speak.

"I married young. I met my wife a few years after college when I was really getting settled into my career. She was pretty, we came from similar backgrounds, had compatible interests, and it seemed like we had a real connection. So after about eight months of dating, I asked her to marry me. I know now that it was a terrible mistake. Looking back, I realize that all the signs were there. Even when we were dating, the sex wasn't great—fairly infrequent, in fact—but I thought that it was just because she was inexperienced and a bit shy. I was sure that once we were man and wife, she would loosen up and we would be able to explore our sexuality together, and discover true intimacy."

Kelli was feeling incredibly sympathetic. She knew exactly what he meant; this sounded so much like her sexless marriage to Paul. Jake paused before resuming.

"It's very important for you to know that it really is about intimacy, in the end…the dynamic connection between two human beings that occurs in mind-blowing sex.

"Anyway, I soon realized after our wedding day that the sex wasn't going to get better after all. In fact, it soon dried up completely. And I do mean *completely*. In our first six months of marriage, we made love less than ten times. At least three of those were on our honeymoon. In the next year or so after that, she let me approach her sexually on two or three special occasions. And the following full year, our third year of marriage, we had sex once, on my birthday. That was it.

"I soon came to realize, to my sorrow, that my wife was…is, I should say…asexual, with virtually no libido or interest in sexual activity. At first I hated her for it, but eventually I understood that she was born that way. She is simply not a sexual creature, in spite of her beauty. Once I saw that this was the case, I couldn't remain angry. For quite a few years, I really thought that I would leave her; I even made plans to do so on several occasions. But in the end, I just couldn't do it. In her own way she loves me, and I love her as I would love a sister, or a dear friend. She is very sweet and kind at times, but there simply is no hint of physicality between us."

Jake paused again and took a sip of water from the glass sitting at his elbow. A few moments of silence elapsed.

Kelli was amazed at his story so far, and the similarities between his marriage and her own. She found herself needing to hear more, so she leaned forward and asked, "So when did the affairs start? Tell me about that."

Jake continued…

"I still remember the moment when I decided to have an affair. We had been married for ten years at that point, and I had fully realized that my wife would not, and could not, be a true sexual partner. However, while I chose to remain in the marriage, I was starting to suffer tremendously. One day, I was walking down the street and saw a beautiful woman in front of me: tall, blond, voluptuous, with long legs in a short skirt. I got an immediate hard-on, one that was so huge and strong that it was physically painful. It had been so long since I had any sexual release, other than my own hand in the shower every day, that I almost came right then and there. I literally wanted to walk up behind this woman, lift her skirt, and take her right there in public, on the street. My sexual feeling and desire for connection was so intense and ravenous that I knew I had to do something about it, or else I was going to go crazy.

"I went straight back to the house I shared with my wife, and jerked off on the couch. I remember my wife was gone, at some yoga class or something…and I literally pleasured myself so hard that I was actually sore and chafed afterwards. More than just the physical sensation, though, seeing that woman made me realize how much I missed and craved sexual intimacy. That was what was absent from my marriage…the incredible connection and intimacy that comes through raw, passionate sexual encounters with another human being. Jerking off had become something that I had to do on a physical level—just to remain sane—but really it wasn't fulfilling anymore. What I really needed was to touch someone else's soul, as I possessed her body.

"In other words, masturbation wasn't cutting it anymore. So once I had spent myself completely, I cracked open my computer and did a search for 'how to have an affair in New Jersey.' I had absolutely no idea what would come up, but I figured it would be something! Maybe a 'How to...' list, a meet-up group, or something. Anything. I was desperate at that point, but I was absolutely amazed at what came up. There were pages and pages of results...testimonials, support groups, and best of all, websites that were devoted specifically to meeting other people who were married, but wanting to enrich their sexual experiences."

Kelli was feeling very odd. How was it possible that his story could so closely mirror her own? While listening to Jake, she was trying to think back to their conversation at the bar. *Had she mentioned anything about going online?* She didn't think so...the more that she thought about it, the more certain she became that she definitely had not discussed her online forays with him. *How could he have had such a similar experience?* Jake's voice brought her back with a start as she realized what he was saying next...

"So I looked at a few different sites, and found one in particular that seemed very promising. It was called www.tsol.xxx, and at first glance it seemed to have just the type of women on it that I was interested in meeting."

At this, Kelli was so startled that she nearly jumped right out of her chair. *OK. This was too weird. Way, way too weird.* Not only was Jake's experience the same as her own, but he had actually gone to the *very same website?* This was too bizarre. A sudden suspicion took hold of her and she couldn't hold it in anymore.

"Did Nina put you up to this?" she blurted out.

Jake stopped mid-sentence and looked at her closely. She couldn't be sure, but it seemed like there was genuine surprise in his eyes. There was also some more of that hidden steel that she had seen earlier.

"Excuse me?" he asked. His tone was soft, yet there was also the faintest hint of annoyance, almost like a warning.

"This is a joke, right? Nina told you?" Kelli was feeling less and less sure of herself.

Jake looked blankly at her. "Nina? Your friend from the bar? Told me what, exactly, Kelli?" He seemed genuinely astounded at her question.

Now she was completely confused, as well as embarrassed. From his reaction, it was obvious that he had no idea what she was talking about. But this also meant that his story must be completely true! Kelli had never felt so bewildered. She tried to cover up her blunder, and let out a nervous little laugh.

"Never mind, never mind. It's nothing. Just, something in what you were saying…never mind. I'm sorry. Carry on."

There was a moment of strained silence, with Jake still gazing intently at her. Kelli thought that she noticed an odd expression flicker across his face, but she couldn't quite identify it.

The moment seemed to go on forever, but just when Kelli felt like she couldn't handle the silence any longer, Jake simply resumed where he'd left off, much to her relief.

"When I first went on the website, I wasn't the man that you see before you today. In fact, I was significantly out of shape, overweight, and put very little stock into my appearance. I wasn't always that way…but you have to understand that my sexless marriage with its lack of passion and desire had really knocked the wind out of me. I had very little sexual confidence left in me at that point. It's strange how it works for a man…even though I knew on an intellectual level that it was my wife's problem, and that she simply had no libido to spend on me, part of me was still deeply wounded and affected by her sexual rejection. As a result, I had really let myself go. I suppose it was a way for me to protect myself.

"Anyway, because I had allowed myself to hide behind excess weight and sloppiness, I spent a month or so on the website before I even met anyone really interesting. But then I had some experiences that seemed really empty, and just based in that same old physical thing...almost like masturbating, with very little intimacy and connection. The lack of passion, combined with the stress of my working life almost caused me to quit the site, right then and there. It just seemed pointless. However, around that time, I met Mai Ling..."

With the mention of Mai Ling, a new tone came into Jake's voice and Kelli quickly glanced up at him. He had an expression on his face that seemed to be halfway between lust and tenderness. Clearly, Mai Ling was someone important.

"Who was Mai Ling?" she asked.

Jake smiled mysteriously. "Ah. Mai Ling comes later. You don't get to hear about Mai Ling today," he responded firmly. "Today is for other things."

"Other things?"

"Yes. You haven't asked me at all about my childhood. Isn't that supposed to be an important part of any therapy session?" His tone was serious, but his green eyes twinkled.

Part of Kelli, the part that was used to arguing with Paul, wanted to point out that this hadn't exactly been a typical therapy session so far. But something about Jake, something in his presence, caused her to hold back. She felt shy around him, like he was an authority figure. She should have been the one in control, but it didn't feel that way.

She smiled back at him. "Ok, then. You're right. It would be good for me to know a little bit more about you…about where you come from and what makes you who you are. Why don't you tell me about that?"

He took another sip of water and spoke again.

"Well, I started my life in the big city, was born in Jersey City. The city has a lot to do with who I am. My younger brother and I were born in an apartment building but moved out when I was very young, just five or six, because of something that had happened there. That event is one of my very earliest memories, and it affected my life in a powerful way."

"What happened?" Kelli asked.

"I saw a man die. And while he died, he looked right at me."

Kelli was mesmerized and a little bit shocked. "Can you tell me a little bit more about that? How did it affect you? For a young child to see something like that…"

"What I remember most is his eyes. I didn't see pain there, or even fear. It was like he was looking straight through me, to the bottom of my being. And somehow, something in me answered him. As if this big, strapping black guy, and me, this little Greek/German kid were brothers. That's really what it was like. Like he was my brother. In that moment, I think that I really understood mortality for the first time.

"I lived in a multistory apartment building; my guess would be that it was about five stories high, containing maybe about thirty units. My family lived on the fourth floor. The apartments lined the rectangular perimeter of the building, and the staircase leading to each floor revolved around the center, forming a central stairwell. It was grueling work, lugging groceries up the rectangular staircase to the fourth floor. One day, I was watching cartoons on a late midweek night. Both my parents worked very late to make ends meet, so I was being watched by an elderly neighbor who always just snoozed in the living room rocking chair while keeping me company.

"I was in the middle of a Loony Tunes episode when I heard police sirens nearby, which was common in my part of Jersey City. They sounded extremely close. I peered out the window to see three police cars. After parking quickly and sloppily in front of the building, four or five officers rushed out of the cars and ran inside. Being my usual curious self, I walked out of the apartment, and looked down the staircase, watching the officers run up each level like military troopers. My heart raced because they were approaching my level. Suddenly they stopped climbing on the level below mine, and ran to the apartment directly underneath. I tiptoed down the staircase; just far enough to peer through the banisters and watch them break into the apartment and quickly run inside the unit.

"All I could remember at that point is one of the officers yelling, 'STOP! HANDS UP!!!' In the next few moments, events seemed to unfold for me in slow motion, as a black man ran out of the apartment towards the staircase. I heard several shots ring out of the apartment, apparently hitting the man. In slow motion, I watched the man crumple and fall onto his face. It only took a few a seconds, but it seemed like minutes. As he fell forward, he looked up and he saw me. His eyes were terrified as he stared at me, piercing my body and soul. I watched him and our eyes held all the way as he slammed onto the concrete floor. In that moment of connection, I felt his soul touch and enter mine. In the next moments, all of the officers ran out of the apartment, and one of them peered up towards me and yelled, 'Get the F** out of here!' I ran back up into my home, trembling and deeply changed.

"I found out later that the ex-wife of the black man had kidnapped his son and tied him in a closet in her apartment. She knew he would come to his rescue, and called the police to report a burglary and frame him while she hid in a friend's unit across the hall to watch him enter. An innocent man had died that day, and I had watched the whole thing. I never forgot that moment of connection with another soul."

"Wow. That sounds...intense," Kelli said, "And what was the aftermath? What lasting effects did that experience have?"

"I remember having nightmares for a long time, mainly about police coming after me. In my dreams, the man who died wasn't necessarily the bad guy; in fact, I identified with him somehow. I think that's why I've always had a certain distrust of authority, and have always wanted to carve out my own path in the world freely. I don't like constraints. I don't like rules. I think that life is for living, and I take what I want."

With this statement, he looked at Kelli, and for an instant she felt like she understood his story about the dying man. It felt like Jake was looking inside her and seeing her most naked, vulnerable self. His story had moved her in ways that she couldn't even begin to express. Somehow knowing that he had been exposed to the grittiness of life at such a tender age made her ache for him, yet it also helped to explain the current of steel and strength that she sensed in him.

"Were there any other experiences like that?"

Jake smiled, but she sensed that there was a lot of emotion hiding behind his eyes. She felt the emotion herself and it moved her. She almost wanted to cry on his behalf.

"Oh, yes. Yes there were. Many of them."

"Such as...?"

"Well, there was the time when a bunch of racist teenagers tied me to a tree and tried to burn me alive. THAT was interesting. If I hadn't been as quick-fingered and alert as I am, I very well could have died in the woods of Kearny, NJ, that day. But I didn't. When I was five years old, my family moved out of Jersey City, to an adjacent blue-collar town called Kearny. At the time, most of the population was Scottish, Irish, Irish/Italian, or just Italian. Then there was me: this darker-skinned, exotic breed. As kids, my siblings and I didn't know or see any difference between our family and other families. In fact, I was always known as the smart, eccentric kid, and based on my surname; most parents assumed that my family heritage was English or something similar. When I played with friends my own age, life was normal.

"However, on the occasions when I was invited over to a friend's home, the situation changed dramatically. Racism was strong in Kearny, and the racist parents of my friends knew right away that I was different. I would often see their reactions immediately in the long, disapproving looks on their faces whenever I entered the home. After they found out more about my different family background, the racism escalated to the point where I wasn't even allowed over. It soon became clear that the entire town was divided along racial and economic lines. On the poor side of town, which ran adjacent to Jersey City and Newark, I never had an issue with racism; I was always treated as family by my friends' parents. However, once we moved to a house on the better, more affluent side of the tracks, my experiences were far more hurtful and lonely.

"The racism I experienced in those years came to a head one day, when I was eleven or twelve. I was walking with one of my friends, one of the few who didn't mind associating with me. We were both outcasts, excluded from the popular, rich circle of young teens in our school. As we were walking, we were spotted by a group of the older rich kids. They started shouting insults at us, and then suddenly, they decided to chase us. It was obvious that their intention was to beat us up just for being different.

"We ran for a while, but they were older and faster. My friend got away, but they eventually caught me in a small wooded area behind a local bank that was used as a cut-through path. This wasn't the first time this had happened, so I was prepared for my usual kicking and beating. I struggled and tried to escape, but this time was different. They held on tight, and then decided to blindfold and tie me to a tree. After I was tied to the tree, the kids laid old branches and leaves around my feet. I could hardly believe what was happening, but it slowly dawned on me that they intended to burn me to death. Using a lighter, they successfully created the fire in the wood and leaves around me.

"At that moment, I truly felt that my life was about to be over. As the flames rose and heated the air that was entering my lungs, the thugs finally ran away from the scene. I struggled as hard as I could and fortunately, their inexperience with rope-tying enabled me to free myself. I limped home and told my parents what had happened. They reported the incident to the police, but this proved to be fruitless. The police were just as racist as everyone else, and they simply wrote it off as childish bullying, without making any arrests. The bullies were never caught or punished, but after that I learned to stay out of their way and to be cautious and careful.

"I drive by the wooded area every once in a while to remind myself how short life is, and how cruel humanity can be. Now that I'm older, as I release the ties from my lover, I will always kiss the tear from her fiery eye, and embrace the passion she gives me when I hold her in my arms unbound."

This time, Kelli couldn't even reply. She was stunned, and just nodded mutely.

Jake continued, "Of course, there was also Catholic school, and the beatings...," He leaned back and laced his fingers behind his head, gazing at Kelli. His tone was musing, almost wistful.

"Uh, what happened there?" She wasn't even sure she wanted to know, but she had to.

He frowned a little, but began to speak again.

He said, "I know exactly where to start. In the Irish-Italian neighborhood where I grew up, the predominant religion was Catholicism.

"Because both my parents worked, they had the money to send me to a private Catholic school in town. It was grueling.

"Most Catholics don't realize that Catholicism stems from Orthodox Christianity. The two religions are very close to each other, with similar masses and communion services. Some of the nuns were very accepting of my religion, but others challenged my loyalty to my religion many times. Although I was given positions of authority and responsibility within the school, such as collecting lunch money, keeping head count, being a crossing guard, etc. the nuns really challenged and criticized my beliefs. Often, as part of their antagonism, they would punish me for no real reason at all.

"One nun in particular, Sister Marie, would come find me when I was working on an essay, or math, or whatever. She would sneak up behind me with one of those old-style long wooden metal-edged rulers, and without warning, would come and hit me on the hand. The reason she gave was always ridiculous; I was holding my pencil wrong, or not sitting up straight, or not doing something the proper way. I still have some of those scars from that ruler on my hands. I have many other scars from playing hockey in school and punching people in the mouth during typical hockey fights, but a good chunk of the scars are from Sister Marie. Luckily, my hands are tan enough that they aren't too visible, but those scars are there.

"Sister Marie kept pushing me and pushing me. I remember one day, when I was about thirteen, it was confession time in school and she asked me if I needed to go to confession. I said no and she challenged me, saying, 'Are you sure? It's been a whole month. You must have sinned at some point.'

"I said, 'No, I really can't think of anything. I don't know if I did anything...I've been pretty good.' That was the truth; I was really a well-behaved guy when I was younger.

"She said, 'You have to think of something.' With that, she forced me to get on my knees in front of this huge cross that was in one of the hallways. She told me to kneel there and think of something, and then ask for God's forgiveness. I knelt there and I was thinking and thinking; she kept yelling at me, 'Come on! Think of something! THINK OF SOMETHING!'

"I couldn't think of anything, and eventually the absurdity of the situation struck me and I couldn't hold in my laughter any longer. 'This is not a joke!' screeched Sister Marie, and she summoned some of the other nuns to join in. Together, one or two of her aged, withered cronies and Sister Marie pushed my head down to the ground in front of the cross and held me there. Sister Marie pulled the back of my pants down. My naked ass was fully exposed, and protruding helplessly as my face was pressed into the ground. I felt vulnerable, exposed, and strangely excited. Sister Marie always carried a cane with her, and I heard it swish against her hand, making a slapping noise.

"She leaned forward next to my face, and said, very forcefully: 'You're a bad, bad boy, Mr. Lapin! And you WILL be punished! You WILL learn your lesson!' She paused for just a moment and I heard the slap of the cane against her hand again. I clenched my cheeks, because I knew what was coming. The first stroke was a complete shock. For just a second I was numb, but then I felt the sting of it spread across my bottom, as it drew the blood to the surface of my soft, exposed skin. I felt a stinging, hot sensation. A few times, she would slap my ass, and massage my whole cheek, to circulate the blood. It hurt like hell, but it also sent warmth through my whole body, and somehow it also aroused me greatly.

"In spite of myself, I felt my cock start to stiffen and then become rock-solid. I'll never know if Sister Marie noticed, but maybe she did. She struck me with the cane again. This time, the heat was even more noticeable. I was trying to wrap my head around the fact that I was getting a major erection. I just hung my head in shame, and hoped that all the nuns around me couldn't see my thick penis pressing upwards into my stomach. Or maybe I wanted them to see my huge manhood.

"Sister Marie gave me twenty or thirty strokes with the cane, and made a few comments about how my suffering would make me appreciate Jesus's suffering on the cross, how my pain would make me a better person, etc. At one point, the pain was pretty bad and I said, 'I don't know why you are doing this to me!'

"Sister Marie replied, 'Because you need to be forgiven.'

"'For what? For what?' I screamed, but she gave me no answer. I wasn't sure if I was screaming in actual pain, or just as a way to hold my orgasm at bay.

"Afterwards, the nuns finally left me alone. I could barely walk, but I remember going to the men's room, touching myself and finally ejaculating, HARD. I was alone, and hated the feeling of self-pleasuring.

"I attended Catholic school from kindergarten through twelfth grade, and my torture at the hands of Sister Marie was constant throughout that time. Once, I was walking in the hallway and she passed me and reached out and punched me in the gut for no reason. Sister Marie liked to pinch, or hit, or kick me, and it often happened when no one was around. After the confession incident, the pain she inflicted would cause that strange arousal again, and would lead to masturbation. I began to understand the link between pleasure and pain in a profound way.

"Sister Marie would threaten me as well, telling me that if I told anyone, she would just call my parents in and tell them that I was lying and making up stories. Of course, because she was a nun, they would believe her, or at least that's what she wanted me to think. She was probably right, too. My parents were very strict and very religious; they would have been unlikely to take my word over that of a priest or nun. That knowledge gave me more pain than the physical torture from Sister Marie.

"As I enter into the BDSM lifestyle, and I administer my punishments and spankings, I always ensure that they are for things that my subs did willfully. Transgressions that we mutually agreed that they wouldn't do and I make them tell me why they are being punished. My subs always have to earn their spankings and punishments. I never punish for things that are beyond their control; e.g., if they are late because they were in an accident, or something else came up that made it impossible for them to complete the task at hand. I would never be upset for those things, or punish them in the same merciless way that Sister Marie punished me. I would always be sure to hold and caress them, and make sure they know that I share in their pain and pleasure, and make sure that we mutually cum afterward. I only punish my subs when they willfully cross my wishes or instructions. In this way, Sister Marie did teach me a very valuable lesson in BDSM: It's never fair to punish for events that are beyond a sub's control. I guess that the beatings I took there just prepared me for how I act later in life in my business relationships."

"Business relationships?"

"That's right. After college, I was involved in several business relationships in which I was subservient to an older, powerful boss. So in both my personal life and in the workplace, I became very skilled at being a submissive, or 'sub.' It's funny how things can shift and change. One of the key lessons I have learned on my journey is the importance of following your heart. Following my heart has made me the man I am today. For example, when I was eighteen, I had a real estate license but struggled. At that age, I couldn't sell a house or even really show a house, because nobody wants to buy real estate from someone so young.

"In any case, at that time there was an Italian restaurant near my house and I used to eat there often. There was a girl who worked at the restaurant who was a little bit older than I was; I was eighteen and she was about twenty or twenty-one. Her name was Amy; we would talk a lot because I would hang out there for a couple of hours at a time. She knew I was struggling as a real estate agent and she told me that she just got a job at a telephone survey place and that they were hiring like crazy, paying top dollar at $12/hr. I followed her there to apply for a job. She ultimately wasn't good at the job, but it turned out that I was. At that place, you really had to be good on the phone. It taught me how to talk to people, to listen to their voice inflections, how to speed up and slow down, and how to manage the inflections of my own voice. This is something that has really affected the way I interact with women. Women love a man who knows how to talk to them and how to whisper those sweet nothings in their ears...

"Anyway, Amy eventually went back to the pizzeria. After about a year, I needed some extra money and they were hiring at the pizzeria, so I ended up working for the telephone survey place during the day and the pizzeria at night. I still had a crush on Amy, but she was older and could get into clubs and bars, and I was still just 18. I had a car, but all of her boyfriends were from the wealthier side of town and drove Corvettes, Camaros, Monte Carlos, etc. while my car was a used Japanese two-door. Still, Amy and I talked a lot and it ended up that I got a job as a dishwasher at the restaurant.

"The place wasn't that busy and as the dishwasher, I could spend hours talking to her. There would be times when it was busy in the front and I'd be in the back washing dishes and have nothing to do, and the two Italian cooks in the back would teach me how to cook. So at the Italian restaurant, I gained another life skill; not only was I learning to talk to people, but the restaurant cooks taught me how to cook meatballs, lasagna dishes, etc. I don't think there's a woman in the world who doesn't think it's really sexy when a man knows how to cook. Because I followed my heart with Amy, I gained that impressive skill.

"I wasn't making quite enough money between the two jobs and as I got older, I started building my IT career. When I was younger, I was always good at computer games, etc., and at one point somebody taught me how to hack phone cards. I did it in a friendly way; I never stole any money or anything like that, but one day the FBI showed up in my living room with my computer sitting on the floor unplugged and taped up. This was back in high school, and at that time the laws were different; you were able to break into company websites and snoop, but the laws today are much stricter. You're not even allowed to break in. Anyway, I didn't get into trouble; they just wanted to talk to me. At that time, the FBI guy told me something very important.

"He asked me, 'Why don't you use your skills to help companies close up their loopholes, rather than sneaking through them?' His words made a huge impact on me, and I remembered that incident when I was working in the kitchen at the Italian restaurant.

"As I was getting closer to the age of twenty-one, I had some skills under my belt, and so I decided to pursue an IT career. Initially, I applied to the Army ROTC program, but because of their testing, even though I was extremely smart and skilled, they wanted me as a frontline soldier. I asked why, and they told me I had a rare eye condition, that allowed me to see through camouflage. This was due to the fact that I had stared at the sun a bit when I was younger, which burned my color filters and actually raised all my other senses. I decided to pass on being a frontline soldier and went into the private sector, becoming the owner of a very successful IT company for about ten years. I can't help but think, had I not burned my filters, would I be dead? A few months after that ROTC recruitment, the U.S. went to war in the Middle East.

"How does this tie in to following your heart? Well, back in high school, when I was learning computers in my freshman year, I had a crush on a girl. She took a typing class, so I took the same typing class just to follow her. Much like I followed Amy later on. I was one of only three guys in the classroom. Our typing teacher liked me and he pushed me, which really helped because I excelled in that class. When I got up to sixty or seventy words per minute, the teacher recommended that I take a second year.

"It turned out that the girl I had followed was sleeping with the whole football team and that kind of turned me off. But in the class there was another girl, who was kind of shy and very pretty. We took the second year of typing class together and bonded for a long time. In that second year, I got up to about eighty-five words per minute, but it was very embarrassing because I was the only guy in the class. There were about six girls, all of whom are secretaries or paralegals today.

"There really wasn't any need for me to take a second year of typing; however, reflecting back now, if I hadn't taken that second year, I wouldn't have aced all my papers in my last year of high school and in college. And I certainly wouldn't be able to type as fast when I blog, email, multitask, etc. as I do today. In my IT career, I definitely needed to have those fast typing skills for typing code, etc.

"Following my heart gave me those essential skills. Looking back, I often think, *Damn! If I didn't follow the girls I had crushes on way back when, I never would have learned how to cook, or how to talk, or how to type.*

"I also followed my heart as far as computers go. My parents were pushing me to be an engineer or a lawyer, but I didn't want to be either of those. I loved computers and technology and still do today. This has been a key part of my success in business, as I am my own IT department in many of my ventures, and that allows me to care for my subs and the women in my life.

"So, things really do happen for a reason if you follow your heart, even though it may not become apparent at the time.

"Coming back around full circle, I ran into Amy, the girl I had a crush on in high school, when I was about twenty-seven and she was thirty. I was now very successful in my IT career, but this was before I got married. We were in a famous club in town and she was with her sister. Her sister had a crush on me, but was a total bitch; in the ten years that I had known them, she hadn't changed one bit. Amy, however, was awesome; she was a total sweetheart. We had kept in touch sporadically throughout those years, from the time I knew her at the pizzeria, when I had my real estate license, and all the way through my IT career. I always stopped by and said hello.

"At twenty-seven, she knew that I had dated a few people already and I was moving on. At the time, I had a girlfriend who I was pretty serious with. I kind of regret it now, because that girlfriend ended up dumping me on my twenty-eighth birthday. I didn't know that at the time, though, and that day in the club, Amy pulled me aside and asked me, 'Why have you never asked me out? We get along so well!'

"I felt like I flashed back to high school; I remember thinking, *Damn, what do I do now; all those female friends that had signed my yearbook, asking the same question.* Little did they know how submissive I was due to the prejudices that existed in town, mainly from the adults. So I simply told her that I was with somebody at the time. Sadly, I knew that the person I was with wasn't with me in her heart. I should have dumped her and told Amy, 'You know, you're right. What are you doing for dinner next Friday?' or something along those lines. That would probably have changed my life, but I didn't do that. I was very faithful, and I'm still very faithful today with my word. When the opportunity is there, go with your heart and follow where it leads. You might not even realize until much later what the importance of that meeting or opportunity was."

Jake's eyes were flashing. Kelli was about to ask more about what he meant by that, but he rushed on before she could interrupt.

"So, there was the racism, the attempt to burn me alive, and the canings from a deranged nun. And then came the day, in early high school, when my best friend at the time, who was older than me, took my virginity, without my consent."

Kelli's jaw had plummeted and she was appalled at what he seemed to be saying. "Are you...are you saying that you were raped, Jake?"

Jake shook his head, slowly. "Well, no. Not exactly. I probably wouldn't use that word. It's not like I was completely unwilling, and I'd be lying if I said that there was no pleasure involved on my end. Let's just put it this way: She was older, and she didn't really give me much say in the matter. It was definitely a situation where she exerted her dominance over me, and I took it."

Kelli was relieved, and relaxed a little. She hadn't even noticed, but her whole body had been tensed as Jake recounted his experiences. The idea of him sleeping with a woman, almost being forced, aroused her and troubled her at the same time.

She asked, "So, how did it happen, exactly? What was the forced situation that caused you to lose your virginity?"

Jake gazed at her and leaned in closer. "Huh uh. I'll tell you, but only after you tell me. You go first."

Normally, Kelli would never share such personal information with a client, but Jake was different. She decided to tell him.

She said: "Growing up, my family situation was not ideal. My father was an alcoholic, and was emotionally neglectful. He never laid a hand on me, or my mother, but he would work long hours, only to come home drunk and pass out on the couch. We barely spoke.

"To escape from my home life, I put all my attention into my schoolwork. I was always a good student, that is...at least until high school. That's when I met Nina, who had moved to my town from California.

"Nina was a true wild child. The whole reason her family had moved was because Nina was showing 'behavioral problems' in her hometown. She started sneaking drinks at the age of twelve, and at the age of thirteen, she was caught in a compromising sexual position with an older teenage boy. Her parents were very conservative and were humiliated by her actions, so they moved her across the country. It didn't do much good, though; Nina was just as wild here as she'd been at home.

"For me, though, Nina was like a breath of fresh air. She freed me from the suffocating atmosphere of my dysfunctional family. From the first day we met, we were best friends and I loved her adventurous spirit. However, she also got me into all kinds of trouble, too. For one thing, when we were sophomores, she convinced me to join the cheerleading squad for the football team.

This led to all kinds of wild house parties.

"Nina was the most flirtatious girl I'd ever seen, and also one of the most aggressively seductive. If she spotted a guy on the football team who she liked, she would seduce him within a week. She was gorgeous, with sexy curves and long, dark curls, so none of the guys ever turned down her advances. After she made a new sexual conquest, she would tell me all about it. I loved hearing all the juicy details and soaked them up, but I was actually pretty shy myself. I did fool around with a couple of guys once or twice, but because of my dad, I didn't drink that much. As a result, I never let things go all the way sexually with anyone.

"That's not to say that I didn't look and fantasize. I was always attracted to very strong, fit men. There were plenty of guys on the football team who caught my eye and quite a few of them pursued me, too. With my long, red tresses; sky-high legs; and tight butt, I was definitely a catch. However, I was also very mature for my age, and even back then, I knew that I wanted more than just a quick fling. I lusted after the football guys but I secretly knew that they were too immature and fickle for me. So I kept myself separated and hoarded my virginity. My classmates knew that I didn't sleep around and I was well respected for it.

"Everything changed in the spring of my senior year when a new guy transferred to our school. His name was Paul. He quickly became one of the most popular students in school. At that time, he was stocky and hyper-masculine, with broad shoulders, tousled brown hair and piercing, ice-blue eyes. From the moment I saw him, I knew I wanted to date him. He was very outgoing and a fantastic football player; he soon became captain of the team.

"He was actually the first guy who ever turned down Nina. She tried her best, but he had eyes for someone else: ME! He would often come up to me at the games, flirting and joking around, picking me up in the air or slipping his arm around my waist. Once, he even slapped my ass as I walked by. I pretended to be shocked and offended, but secretly I was flattered.

"Prom time rolled around, and one day Paul approached me as I was leaving school.

"'Hey, Kells,' he said, leaning against a locker. I could smell his cologne; it was something musky.

"'Hi, there, Paul.'

"He didn't waste any time. 'So, do you have a date to the prom?' Paul was always like that. Direct. Straight to the point.

"'Uh, no. Why?'

"'Because I'm going to take you.' He grinned, almost suggestively.

"I was a little bit flustered. 'Um, OK!' I smiled up at him. He tipped my chin up and brought his face close to mine. Just for a few seconds. Then he turned and walked away without a word.

"I was thrilled. I was headed to the prom with the football captain! Little did I know that would change my life forever...

"Prom night finally arrived. I had never felt more beautiful or excited as I left the house. My dress was a shimmery, blue, off-the-shoulder number, and I had pinned matching flowers in my auburn ringlets. I paid more attention to my makeup than ever before, smoothing on shimmery blue shadow and pink lip gloss.

"When Paul picked me up, he gave me a quick look over, and then waved me into his car. Before we had even gone a block, he handed me an open beer.

"'Paul...I...won't we get in trouble?'

"'Don't worry about it, hun. Tonight we're gonna party!'

"I don't remember all that much about the actual dance. I know that

Paul and I did dance together, but what I remember most is the number of drinks that he brought me. There were chaperons, but Paul had a big plastic bottle full of vodka that he had snuck in, and he kept adding it to the punch. I had never really been drunk before so it really snuck up on me. Before I could slow down, the room was spinning and I could only remember portions of the conversations I had with people.

"Before I knew it, the night was over. I wasn't really aware of what was going on, but I remember that Paul came up to me and grabbed me around the waist from behind, nuzzling my neck.

"'C'mon, babe…let's go out to the car.'

"The memory of what followed is blurry even to this day. That night, while I was almost too drunk to stand, Paul took my virginity in the back of his Thunderbird. I remember a sharp stabbing pain and that he was rough with me. I know now that his roughness was due to his own level of inexperience, not because of any malice. It was almost date rape, but not quite, because I do remember petting heavily with Paul in the car and then him asking me, 'Wanna do it?'

"I answered, 'Yes.' Although in retrospect I didn't really know what I was doing, I did know that I genuinely liked Paul. He was handsome, popular, strong…all the qualities that appealed to me. I do remember the sex being somewhat mechanical, very robotic. I thought it was me, just being drunk and silly, but throughout our marriage, he has always been that way.

"Afterwards, Paul drove me home, gave me a kiss goodnight, and left.

"We 'went steady' after that. Sex with Paul was a huge disappointment to me, though, and it didn't improve much after the first time. He would thrust into me a few times, roughly, then cum within a few minutes. It was very, very mechanical. All the dreams I'd had as a young girl about romance and tenderness began to disappear.

"I would have broken things off with Paul sooner, but a few weeks after prom I realized that I had missed my period and a test revealed that I was pregnant. When I told Paul he was white-faced with fury, but to his credit, he told me that he would support me and the baby if I decided to keep it. I did want to keep the baby, but our parents put a lot of pressure on both of us to NOT get married, but to seek an abortion instead. We talked about it, and decided to keep the baby as my parents were very strict religiously, but Paul's parents disowned him. So six months after prom, we tied the knot in a little ceremony in front of a justice of the peace. Three months later, our first beautiful daughter, Kaitlyn, was born.

"Those early years were rough; Paul and I both had to delay college in order to seek out livings. Paul worked nights as a janitor and days as a line cook while we continued to try and save money. My parents helped me watch the baby, and helped pay my way through college, as it was obvious I would be the bread winner in our marriage. Eventually things did get better, but I'm not sure that he ever really forgave me for getting pregnant.

"And the sex? Nothing much ever changed there. Paul and I had rushed through the wedding due to my pregnancy; I remember it like it was yesterday. A woman's wedding day is supposed to feel special and exciting, but there was none of that for me.

"Paul was also beginning to show his true colors; he spoke harshly to me many times throughout the wedding planning and seemed to have no interest whatsoever in anything that I suggested. I was devastated. Deep down, I knew that this was the real him. Being so young, though, I didn't feel that I had any other option but to marry him, especially with the pressure coming from our parents.

"In any case, the wedding day itself passed in a blur. I remember walking up the aisle to Paul and instead of feeling happiness, feeling a heavy knot in the pit of my stomach. I remember my family members looking at me condescendingly and staring at my stomach. It was not a day of joy; it was a day of faint humiliation.

"However, my family had grouped together and decided that we needed to have a honeymoon. They decided to send us on a week-long cruise to Antigua, in the Caribbean. I felt like the time together would bring Paul and me closer; how could it not? We were going to have a family together, after all.

"The night before the cruise started, we spent our wedding night in a hotel. Even though we had a shotgun wedding prior, I still wanted the experience to be special. So I bought some beautiful white lingerie and set up candles all around the room along with a bottle of wine for us.

"Like much of what would follow in our marriage, it was a huge disappointment. We arrived at the room late in the evening, and both of us were exhausted. But I gathered up my strength and asked Paul to take a shower. My plan was to set up the room while he was in there.

"Paul agreed. He went into the bathroom and shut the door. However, as he walked in, I noticed that he was carrying something. It looked like a magazine. He was holding it in a strange way, almost as if he were hiding it from me. After he closed the door to the bathroom, I heard the water start running.

"My head was spinning. *What the fuck did he take into the bathroom with him?* I had a crazy, nagging suspicion that I knew, but I couldn't accept it.

"The water continued to run, a steady, uninterrupted stream. I intuited that he hadn't even gotten into the shower yet. Finally, I couldn't take the curiosity and suspicion anymore.

"'Paul, honey? Sorry, but I need to grab something quickly.' Before he had a chance to answer, I opened the bathroom door quickly.

"There was my husband of just a few hours, sitting on the toilet. He was holding his swollen dick in his hand, stroking it rapidly. The strained, flushed expression on his face made it obvious that he was only a short time away from cumming. In his other hand was a porn magazine. My new husband wasn't getting ready for our wedding night; he was jerking off to porn!

"I was completely shocked and simply slammed the door shut. *What the fuck? WHAT THE FUCK?*

"I stumbled to the bed and sat there, staring down at my hands. *So much for our wedding night.* Paul hadn't even stopped when he saw my look of horror; he just kept going. This was the man I had married.

"There was something else that was nagging at my mind. That porn mag...why did he need that?

"The next day, we began our cruise.

"Paul and I hardly spoke the day after I caught him with his pants around his ankles. I had sobbed quietly to myself, alone in bed, and then pretended to be asleep when he finally came out of the bathroom. He didn't say a word to me or touch me; he just crawled into the other side of the bed and was snoring within minutes.

"I was feeling nauseated because of the pregnancy and immediately knew that being on a ship wasn't going to help any. I spent the first day or two in the cabin, heaving. That didn't stop Paul, though. He was out basking in the sunshine next to the pool, sipping on cocktails all day long.

"When he did finally come back to the cabin, he started telling me all about some new friends he had met.

"'Kelli, you gotta meet Steve and Lauren,' he said. 'They're incredible. We're having so much fun. Wanna join us for dinner tonight?'

"I didn't, but I was sick of sitting around feeling ill, so I agreed to venture out.

"Lauren was a sleek blonde, with bright blue eyes and breasts that were obviously not her natural size. They were gigantic. I disliked her immediately. It wasn't her looks—I wasn't that shallow—it was the way she moved, like every gesture was a calculated seduction. I also didn't like the way she fawned all over Paul. I could tell right away that she was going to be trouble.

"Her husband, Steve, was not much better. He was slick and smooth, with the classic personality of a politician. He started flattering me the second he met me.

"'Oh, Paul didn't tell us you were hot,' he commented, while holding my hand for just a little too long.

"'Oh? How surprising.' I tried to sound cool and distant.

"Just then, Lauren sidled up next to me. 'No, he sure didn't.' She giggled as she laid her hand on my arm. I was startled at the familiarity.

"Steve laughed, and then murmured something in Lauren's ear. I couldn't quite hear what it was.

"I didn't feel very comfortable, physically or emotionally. Paul seemed unnaturally close with this couple somehow. *What is going on?*

"As the evening progressed, all three of them drank heavily. Obviously, I stuck to soda water with lemon. Being sober, I could see how things were progressing. Lauren laughed, batted her eyelashes, and flipped her hair back and forth over her shoulder constantly. She was wearing a strapless top, and as the night went on, it slipped farther and farther down, showing most of her cleavage. It was also obvious that she wasn't wearing a bra; her nipples were clearly outlined. I could tell from how both men looked at her that she was arousing them. At one point, she placed her hand on Paul's knee. She leaned in close to him, talking in a low tone while her hair fell forward and hid them both from view. I could see Paul's erection, his cock stiffening, and the sight made me feel sick again.

"I was about to excuse myself when I looked up and saw Steve staring at me. He was smiling, and there was an invitation in his smile. When I met his eye, he turned, looked at Lauren's hand stroking Paul's leg, and then back to me. I didn't know what was happening, or didn't want to admit it to myself.

"'Excuse me, I'm...I'm really not feeling well. I'm going to go back to the cabin.'

"I stood up and waited for a moment. Steve kept staring, and then he finally looked away with a bored expression. As for Paul? He didn't even look up, or notice I was gone.

"I went back to the cabin and cried into my pillow again. Paul did come home that night, but not until 4 a.m.

"The next night, he didn't come home at all. When I confronted Paul about not coming home to our cabin, he was hostile and defensive.

"'I was out with Steve and Lauren, hon. We were just having fun and ended up staying at the bar until five or six o'clock.'

"'Five or six o'clock? It's 11 a.m. and you just got here ten minutes ago.'

"'Jesus, Kelli! Do I seriously have to explain every little thing to you? Their cabin was a million miles closer than ours is to the bar, so they let me crash on their floor. I was too smashed to know the difference. Probably wouldn't have even made it here without passing out.'

"'Great, Paul. Just great. Thank you so much.'

"With that, I stormed out of the cabin and blindly rushed down the hallway. I was trying to hold it together and avoid bursting into tears, but I couldn't keep the flood from coming. I just needed fresh air. I found my way out onto a balcony that looked over the sea, and then let myself dissolve into sobs. *What was I thinking? Why did I think that this would be OK?* I knew that Paul wasn't the greatest guy; I always had. *Why did I let our parents talk us into this marriage? How am I going to survive it?* All of these questions and feelings and more rushed through my head.

"I looked at the blue, blue sea stretching out in the wake of the cruise ship. It looked so peaceful, so inviting. For one brief second, I saw myself climbing onto the railing, and then just letting go, floating down to the water, and then drifting away.

"In that moment, there was one thing that pulled me back down to Earth and kept me from going any further: my baby. A kick in my belly pulled my thoughts back from the water. It was the first time I felt my daughter move, and I couldn't believe it. I gasped with delight and cupped my hands around my stomach. I had a reason to live.

"Years later, it was my brush with suicide that prompted me to pursue a career in therapy. I wanted to help people however I could. Of course, getting into sex therapy was another journey, a story for a different time. But the initial move into the mental health care field came from that one desperate moment, standing on the cruise ship, gazing into the deep blue ocean.

"When I found my way back to the cabin several hours later, Paul was waiting for me. He had a sheepish, guilty look on his face.

"'Look, Kelli,' he said. 'I don't want things to be weird with us, okay?'

"I felt cold as ice. 'Paul, you stayed out all fucking night with those creeps.'

"He flinched. 'Steve and Lauren? Nah. They're good people. We had a great time, and I wish you would have been with us.'

"He looked at my face, and then his tone changed. 'But, look, sweetie. With the baby coming and everything, I don't want to rock the boat, you know? So I'm sorry. That's what I'm trying to say.'

"Young as I was, I believed him. The rest of the cruise passed without incident, and I found myself believing against hope that maybe I could have a life with Paul after all.

"That was always the thing about Paul...the thing that kept us married for many more years. He always apologized...until the next time. I was too innocent and naïve to know that his apologies were just as empty then as they would be years down the road."

"Wow," said Jake, "that's definitely one hell of a prom experience! I'm happy to say that mine was a lot more enjoyable."

"Oh really? So what was your prom night like?"

"It was amazing, but that's a story for a different time."

Jake's tone shifted now. "So combine all of those experiences with a few other betrayals from work colleagues, with my failed marriage, etc. and you can understand how my self-confidence was pretty much at an all-time low by the time I joined that website."

He grinned. "That's all changed now, though. As I mentioned before, I don't think that anyone could really say that I have low confidence at this point."

Kelli couldn't help but respond to his warm smile with a grin of her own. She glanced at the clock and was shocked to realize that as he had told his story, time had elapsed without her noticing its passing. It was already 5:00 p.m. The session was over.

Reluctantly, she cleared her throat and said, "Well, it's 5 p.m. But

I'm glad that we covered some good ground in this session. I think it's important for us to get to know each other and feel comfortable."

To her surprise, Jake started chuckling in reaction to her comment. His eyes twinkled, and he said, "Oh, yes. Yes, it is." Then his laugh ceased and there was a dramatic pause. "Now, tell me why you were late today."

Kelli felt herself blushing and looked down at her hands on her lap. "Well, I stepped out to get a chai, and I thought I had enough time, but I didn't. I really do apologize for that."

Jake stood up and walked over to her. She remained seated, but could feel the warmth of his body just a few feet away, looming over her. It made her feel small, feminine, and intensely sexual.

When he spoke, his voice was low and firm. "You thought you had time, huh? I bet you often make that mistake…thinking you have enough time."

She didn't respond; the closeness of his body was making her feel crazy. She was afraid that if she moved, he would smell her arousal.

Jake moved back a few steps suddenly, and then spoke again, "Kelli, I need you to stand up and get a piece of paper and a pen."

Again acting with surprising obedience, she did as she was told, feeling the vibration of his words echo through her entire physical being. She got the pen and paper, and stood before him.

"Now, I want you to write this down, exactly as I dictate it. Will you do that?"

She nodded, and then remembering, said, "Yes."

"'I, Kelli Lemberg, understand that I will not be late for my sessions with Jake Furie Lapin," Jake spoke slowly and surely. Kelli couldn't quite believe what she was doing, but she wrote down his words.

Many clients had odd requests. This was all just part of her job, that's all.

Jake continued, "If I, Kelli, am late, I will receive my discipline. This discipline will consist of five strokes on the bottom administered with a belt. I will accept this as my just punishment and discipline for tardiness."

Kelli was frozen for a brief, thrilling second. Was Jake asking her to accept a *spanking* from him? The second the thought entered her mind, she realized how much it turned her on in spite of herself. She thought of Paul, and how weak he was...how goddamn *weak*. And here was this virile, sexual man stating that he would take control and would discipline her if she disobeyed or stepped out of line.

She finished writing what he had told her to write. "Do I sign it now?" she asked, huskily. She was sure that he must hear the arousal in her voice.

"Yes. You sign it."

She did.

{ 4 }

The following Monday found Kelli in her office at 3:50 p.m. looking with anticipation at the door. The week had crawled by. At several points over the past seven days, she had found herself tempted to pick up the phone and call Jake under the auspices of "checking in." Fortunately, each time she picked up the phone she realized how foolish that would be and restrained herself. Instead, she counted down the days, hours, and moments until their next appointment.

Her intercom buzzed and she nearly jumped out of her skin. *God, I'm high-strung these days!* she mused and picked up the phone, "Yes?"

"Your four o'clock is here. Shall I send him in?"

"Yes, thanks."

She placed the phone on the receiver and whipped out a tiny hand-held mirror from her desk drawer, giving herself a quick once-over. *Food in teeth? No. Makeup perfectly applied? Yes.* She had just replaced the mirror when the door opened and Jake entered the room.

Today, his suit was a dark charcoal, and he was wearing a deep red, silk shirt that perfectly complemented his olive skin and startling green eyes. His tie was a tasteful grey with red and cream accents, and he wore the same heavy, burnished silver cufflinks that she had noticed the week before. Taking him in, Kelli felt her breath catch. For a moment, she didn't trust herself to speak, but she drew on her reserves of strength and calmed her voice. When she opened her mouth, she was pleased to hear that she sounded steady and professional.

"Hello, Jake. How are you?"

He smiled that dazzling smile, and she felt her knees go weak. She gripped the edge of her desk, trying to look casual.

"I'm fine, Kelli," he said. "Shall we begin?" He strode across the room and took the same chair in which he had sat before, Kelli's therapist chair. She sat across from him, conscious of the way that his eyes took in her skirt and shapely legs. She was wearing the ensemble he required, the shirt and skirt that she had begun to think of as *his* shirt and skirt, *his* outfit. She wore it, but it belonged to *him*.

Drawing out the yellow legal pad that she used to make notes during client sessions, she positioned herself a little more comfortably in the chair. "OK, so in our last session…you told me about watching a man die." Jake nodded. "But there is one thing that troubled me. You said that this was not the only time you saw a man die. Did you mean that there have been other deaths that you have witnessed?"

"Yes," Jake answered, "There have."

Kelli nodded encouragingly, and Jake began:

"Well, at the tail end of my college career I took on a job in electronics in a neighboring town in order to make a little bit of extra cash. It was during the winter, and, initially, it was a great place to work. I learned to install car radios, which I loved. One winter evening, at the time of year where it gets dark early, between four thirty and five o'clock, I was working on a car. The location of the electronics place was on the corner of two streets, and there was no car port, garage, or anything like that. People would just park their cars outside the place and we'd work on them there. As it happened, there were a lot of drug deals that went down on that corner and a few really bad incidents had occurred."

"Why? What was happening to cause these situations?" Kelli was curious. She couldn't believe how polished and masculine he was, how confident. How could anyone who had experienced such things be so calm? It was truly amazing.

"Well, it was because the drugs being sold weren't any good, there wasn't enough money to pay, etc. I really don't know why or how things went wrong because I wasn't involved, but I vividly remember what happened that day. It was getting dark, twilight, and there was a transaction going down between a scrawny little guy and a thuggish drug dealer who I recognized from around the neighborhood. The deal took an ugly turn for whatever reason, and the dealer pulled out a gun and stuck it in the scrawny guy's face. When that happened, the guy turned…and in that moment, our eyes met. I saw his terror, but before I could even register what was happening, the dealer pulled the trigger. Without saying a word, he blew him away right on that street corner. I was working on a car and I saw the whole thing."

Kelli winced. She couldn't believe that Jake had seen more than one person get killed. She wanted to reach out and touch him, to reassure him, but she restrained herself. "What did you do?"

"Well, as soon as the shot happened, I just crouched down and hid there, terrified because obviously I was a witness. I stayed there, hiding, and the drug dealer ran away without seeing me."

"Did you tell anyone what you'd seen?"

"I told the owner that I had seen something and he just told me to keep my mouth shut. Nonetheless, it was obvious that job was in a dangerous environment. I called in sick the rest of that week, and then I told the owner that witnessing the event had left me too shaken to continue working there. He was actually extremely upset and called me a pussy, a weakling, scaredy-cat, etc. I told him that being in an environment where I could be blown away that quickly and easily was something that I really didn't want to do, so I gave up that job. To this day...I just remember the look in that man's eyes. That connection...it was unlike anything else, except for what happens during the most intimate lovemaking."

Kelli asked, "So, between those two events—the time when you were really young and this time at the electronics store—were those the only times you saw someone die?"

"No, there was one other. In the town where I grew up, a really good friend of mine was hooked on heroin. I used to hang out with him after school, and we would play poker or role-playing games. I always knew when he shot up because he would get up and disappear into the bathroom or his bedroom and come back high. He knew that I didn't really approve, but that didn't affect our friendship. Almost everyone in our group of friends really respected me for the fact that I was pretty clean. Even though there was a lot of heroin and pot in that town, I always kept clear of that stuff. My friend's name was Billy..."

Jake's voice trailed off and Kelli saw that his eyes had a faraway look. She prodded him gently, "What happened to Billy?"

"Well, one time he did his usual thing, where he disappeared into his room and shot up his heroin. Only this time, when he came out of his room he wasn't his usual dozy self. He came stumbling out and his eyes were wide open, bulging out of his face. He stared at me, and just like with those other two men, our eyes met and connected in this incredible, heart-wrenching way. Billy's shirt was off and his heart was racing so hard that you could actually see it pumping, pushing his skin outward, and he was screaming and waving his arms around. After a few seconds, he just collapsed and fell face forward on the floor. After he fell down, we saw that his back was this weird grayish blue color, almost like bruises. It actually looked like someone had punched him repeatedly in the back."

"Did you call 911?" Kelli couldn't imagine what it must have been like for Jake to see his friend in such trouble.

"Yes, of course we called 911. An ambulance came, but it was too late. He died that day. When they did the autopsy, they told us that basically he had taken a hot dose of heroin—the heroin was laced with toxic speed—and his heart had exploded. When it exploded, it was with such ferocity that it actually bruised his back. That's what we had witnessed. It was really unfortunate and tragic. He was a really nice guy who just got caught up in the drug scene. The way he looked at me in those last moments…I mean, that's stayed with me all these years, for sure. I realized that the eyes are the windows to the soul, and in those moments, I really saw into the souls of other human beings."

Kelli was amazed. "It sounds like you really cared about these people you saw die. What an amazing thing. What about your other friends? Can you describe the people you grew up with in the town?"

"Well, the town was mostly Scottish, Irish, and Italian. There was definitely a huge Scottish and Irish presence in particular. For example, I remember fish and chips being a very popular meal and the big thing in town. I was definitely the oddball with my dark skin and exotic background. It was weird; I grew up on the 'bad' side of town, the poor side of the tracks, a very poor blue-collar neighborhood. Later in life, we moved to the white-collar part of town. It was rough growing up because everybody was Irish/Italian and blond or strawberry blond, with fair skin and freckles, and here I was, the dark-skinned kid…the outsider. When I was younger we didn't know any difference, and just wanted to have fun playing dodgeball and horsing around. I had a lot of good friends and good times."

"It sounds like your environment had a big impact on you," Kelli mused. "I'd really like to hear more about that." She smiled at him, and he smiled back.

"Yes, it did. The defining moments, though, were when I was invited over to people's homes. As you would expect, it was common for kids to get invited for lunch, snacks, or whatever. However, my friends quickly learned not to invite me over in the same way. When they did, their parents would look at me strangely; they knew I wasn't like them, and they would covertly encourage the kids to shun me or push me away. Socializing with me was seen as socializing with one of the 'bad guys.' That really hurt, mainly because it really stopped me from having relationships with girls. As a result, I didn't really have any kind of relationship or companionship with the opposite sex until I got to college, after I had moved out of the town."

"So you had no female intimacy at that point?"

"Well, I think I mentioned last time that in high school there was an incident with a friend of mine, Elaine. She was a few years older—I was a freshman at the time—and she took my virginity, somewhat by force as part of a role-playing game. I went along with it, but it was an odd situation."

Kelli blinked. "Yes. I remember. It sounded forceful. Do you want to tell me more about that?"

Jake smiled, almost amused, but with an unmistakable note of regret, "I'm sure you would love to hear all about it," he teased, but then his face got serious. "In all honesty, no, I don't. There is too much emotion connected with that, too much unresolved history. Elaine still haunts me. Around the time I entered high school, I had become very interested in role-playing games. Of these, Dungeons and Dragons was my favorite. I used to play it regularly with some of my closest friends.

"My character was a Demi-Elf named Mikkal. Demi-Elves are half-human and half-Elf; in other words, they have a dual nature. This fit my own personality perfectly. As I got older, I realized that there were two sides battling against each other inside me. The first side of me was like the elves: compassionate, highly intelligent, quick-witted, physically nimble, and reserved. The other side was very human: prone to taking risks, being reckless, and disregarding danger.

"One late, rainy Thursday afternoon, my friends and I arranged to meet at a D&D gathering. However, three of my male friends had been put into detention at school for engaging in horseplay during gym class. As a result, the only two people who attended our gathering were Elaine O'Conner, whose house we were meeting in, and myself.

"Elaine was a junior, but she had been held back a year in elementary school, so she should have been a senior. Since I had started school a year early, there was a three-year age gap between us. Our mothers had met through school activities and were friends. Elaine's mom was divorced and, unlike other parents in town, had no problem with my racial background so I had spent a lot of time at her house while growing up. All through elementary and middle school, Elaine was like an older sister to me. A sister I never had.

"Recently though, I had started to become aware of how beautiful she was. Somehow I had never noticed before. Elaine and I decided to engage in a little bit of one-on-one role play while we waited for the others to get out of detention. We always had our gatherings in her bedroom, and this day was no different. The room was already dim because of the rainy weather, but Elaine drew the curtains, dimmed her overhead light to a faint glow, and lit candles throughout the room—a D&D ritual.

"Elaine took on the role of Dungeon Master for the session. Her character was a full-blood Elf named DM Zorra. As Dungeon Master, she told my character, Mikkal, that he encountered a female Elf demi-god who put him under a spell of binding. With that, DM Zorra lit a few extra candles and then she bound my wrists with a silken rope as a way of enhancing the role play. Then she instructed Mikkal to lie down on the bed. The female Elf demi-god wished to punish Mikkal for being too close to humans, but as a half-human himself, Mikkal appealed the punishment.

"'Absolutely not,' replied the female demi-god. 'You have transgressed and you WILL receive your punishment.'

"With that, she declared that Mikkal's punishment would be five lashes on the chest.

"'Remove your shirt, Mikkal,' she said. I, as Mikkal, obeyed with a sensation of fear and excitement mingled together.

"Elaine, or DM Zorra, then bound my hands to the bedposts more securely. She opened a drawer and withdrew a long strip of satin, which she wrapped around my eyes.

"I felt my breath quicken.

"'Now hold still,' said Elaine.

"After Elaine prompted me to remain still, I heard the sound of a drawer open and then felt an incredible sensation on my chest and nipples. Elaine had withdrawn a long leather crop, and was teasing me with the tassels. She drew them back and forth across my erect nipples and the feeling was unlike anything I had ever experienced before.

"I was half-expecting her to snap the whip suddenly and make me sting, but she didn't. Instead, I suddenly felt her breath against my ear.

"Speaking as DM Zorra, Elaine whispered, 'Mikkal, have you been with a woman yet?'

"Trembling, I responded, 'No, DM.'

"I knew that Elaine had a reputation for promiscuity even though until this point she had just been a friend to me—almost like a sister. I had heard the rumors, though, and she even told me about a few of her sexual encounters. I knew that she had a certain 'type' that she liked, and I wasn't it. However, she told me later that she was intrigued by my body, as it was so different from those of the boys she usually dated.

"In any case, I was still blindfolded but I felt her softly kissing my face. She started by kissing each cheek softly, then my forehead and chin. The softness and wetness of her mouth really turned me on and I moaned slightly and parted my lips. She teased me for a while and then finally laid her mouth against mine. I had kissed girls before, but Elaine was something totally different. She knew exactly what she was doing as she pulled and teased my lower lip, flicking her tongue inside my mouth expertly.

"Things were already heating up for me, but then Elaine began her descent on my body. She kissed around the line of my collarbone and neck, and then down the curve of my chest, following the crease in the middle of my abs. My nipples were rock hard, and she flicked her tongue over each one several times before continuing south.

"She reached my waistline and ran her tongue into my navel before unzipping my fly. My cock was throbbing hard at this point. I didn't even have time to question what was happening before she pulled both my boxers and pants off completely, leaving my erection completely exposed.

"She took the crop and ran the leather tassels over my groin area, dipping them into the creases of my legs and flicking them across the length of my cock lightly. I moaned again.

"Elaine spoke. Her voice sounded throaty. 'Mmmm…Mikkal…you are quite a bit larger and thicker than those Irish boys I've seen before, and circumcised!' With that, she ran her hand over my swollen penis and then spoke the words that changed my life:

"'Today, Mikkal, you will be christened. By me.'

"I then felt a completely new sensation: warm, wet, and ecstatic.

Elaine was going down on me. She wrapped her mouth around my erection, stroking it with her full lips, running her tongue up and down my shaft and over my balls.

"It's a miracle that I didn't cum right then and there in her mouth, but somehow I held out. Physically, the sensation was incredible. Emotionally, I was a little bit bewildered and confused; I didn't know quite what was happening or what I should do, but I was willing to let Elaine—or DM Zorra—have her way with me.

"After a few minutes, the sensation changed once again. The warmth and wetness around my cock shifted in a completely new way. I felt Elaine's hands against my chest and her legs wrapped around the outside of mine. I suddenly realized that she was riding me and my cock was inside her pussy.

"Elaine must have felt me trembling, because she said in a sensual whisper, 'Don't panic, Mikkal. Just stay focused. Don't lose control; don't let go until I tell you.'

"A few minutes later I heard her breathing quicken and felt her whole body tense against mine.

"'NOW, Mikkal!' she shrieked, as I felt her pussy pulse wildly against my cock. I let go just then and came hard. Extremely hard.

"Afterwards, I felt a little bit lost.

"'Elaine…is everything OK? What just happened?'

"She reached down, loosened my blindfold, and kissed me lightly on the cheek.

"'Don't worry about it, Jake,' she said and smiled at me. She was Elaine again, not DM Zorra. Then she helped me get dressed, as I asked what this all meant. Elaine smiled and ignored the question.

"'No, seriously Elaine, what does this all mean?'

"'Well, it means that until I graduate and go to college, we're partners. That's all. Is that OK with you?'

"I nodded mutely and headed home shortly afterward.

"Sadly, my relationship with Elaine was fated to be short. A few weeks after our first encounter, Elaine discovered that she was pregnant and she believed that the baby was mine.

"Her mother was furious and even angrier when she heard that I was the father. She forbade us from seeing each other. Word got around town, though, and Elaine and her mother soon moved away.

"The incident with Elaine affected me deeply. She had taken my virginity, and had done so in a dominant way that had left me little choice. I was unsure how to handle myself around women, which led to a very limited dating life. I didn't even have a date to my junior prom. Strangely enough, when I look through my yearbook, I see notes from girls who clearly had crushes on me. But, I was too unsure of myself to recognize it at the time."

Kelli asked, "Did you ever find out what happened to Elaine?"

Jake nodded. "Yes. As I mentioned, she moved away with her mother shortly after finding out that she was pregnant. Her mom eventually threw her out of the house. She was dating a loser named Sharky. We both used to go to a park that was between our two towns and make out or have casual sex. This went on for a few years in total, until I graduated high school, which she never did finish, I thought ironically.

"One thing about Elaine was that she had a shark tattoo on her shoulder. I always assumed that it was for her boyfriend, Sharky. However, she divulged to me one day that the shark tattoo was actually for me! I couldn't believe it, and asked her to explain. She told me that she had told others in school about the scar on my arm. She told them that I encountered a shark at Wildwood; I wrestled with the shark and prevailed. It was amazing. It's funny because she spread the rumor around and even though it wasn't true, a lot of people believed it. So I was pretty happy about that when she told me.

"One thing about Elaine I had to admit was that she was masterful at controlling sex."

"In what way?" Kelli curiously asked.

"I always remember Elaine had a way of pinning me down, taking me inside her mouth, and losing control. She loved riding me, riding me hard, especially reverse; she would straddle me, grab my legs, and just kept pounding me and pounding me, amazed at how big I was and how long I could last.

"In the end, she didn't marry Sharky, thankfully. He wasn't very good to her. We kept in touch for a long time, and last I heard she was happy and doing well as a single mom, raising her child."

Kelli was happy to hear it. "Great! Go on," she said.

"Growing up in that town, there wasn't anyone who was like me physically, in the sense of my ethnicity. There certainly weren't other girls who looked like me. They were all very different. Throughout my whole life, I've been a product of that environment, in that I've found myself attracted to a particular type of woman: Scottish, Irish, and also a fair number of Italian women. That's what I grew up with and who I saw around me all the time. There have been women of other ethnicities who were attracted to me and approached me at various times, but I generally shunned them or rebuffed them, mainly because I just didn't know how to react or behave around them. I realize now, as an older man, how stupid that was. These days, I always keep an open mind as far as relationships go and treat everyone equally. But racism was such a part of the town where I grew up that it really did affect me and cause me to be attracted to a certain type of woman, even while they pushed me away, which hurt and scarred me."

Jake paused slightly and took a sip of water. Kelli jotted down a few notes on the legal pad and then asked, "So how did you change your mind and open up to other types of relationships?"

"I was fortunate; I graduated fourth in my class and went away to school in Boston. As a freshman, my room assignment wasn't given to me until just a week before school started. As a result, I was placed in a dorm that was mostly occupied by juniors and seniors, even though my best friend was also a freshman and was placed in the freshman dorm. Initially, I led a typical freshman life. My freshman friend would take me to freshmen parties, the typical keg parties with a huge keg of beer in the basement, people getting hammered, and a guy/girl ratio of about twenty to one. In other words, a freshman guy was extremely lucky if he was able to hook up at the end of the night. I guess that the girls were lucky in that they had their choice of guys. I was still pretty shy and reserved, and I certainly never got lucky at any of those parties."

"Really?" she asked. "No hook ups?" She found it hard to believe that someone as sexy as Jake wouldn't have fooled around with a lot of women.

"No. Not even once.

"However, I was fortunate in that I was living in the dorm with mostly juniors and seniors, and they would take me to more 'adult' parties. Those parties were a lot more structured; there would be no more than twenty or thirty people, with an equal ratio of men to women. The idea was that everybody would be able to hook up by the end of the evening. My shyness still held me back, though. I was intimidated by the older girls. Because I was a freshman, there was a maturity gap with these girls who were two or three years my senior, and I didn't know how to approach or speak to girls in general, much less those who were older and more sophisticated.

"However, as fate would have it, it was at one of these parties full of older people that I had my first real experience interacting sexually with a woman. I was at a party hosted by a junior and I was sitting on a loveseat against one wall of the room. The hosts had created a drink called the 'Hell in a Melon.' It was one of those creative, sugar-filled inventions that only college-aged kids come up with. Basically, the hosts took a watermelon, cut it in half, hollowed it out, and then filled it with a mixture of blueberry Kool-Aid and grain alcohol. I was a complete light-weight at that time and wasn't really aware of the potency of the grain alcohol. The drink was actually pretty good, like a tasty and potent fruit punch. I drank two or three glasses of it and just sat there on the loveseat and got really, really, really buzzed."

"Did anyone catch your eye there? Any women?" Kelli asked.

"Oh yes. There was a Latina girl who really caught my eye; she was outgoing, talking to everyone around her, and very pretty, with amazing eyes. At one point, I asked someone who she was and was told that it was her house and that she was the hostess. I also remember noticing her full breasts and hips, lusting for her, and feeling my penis get stiff inside my jeans. As I got more intoxicated, I remember noticing everyone around me hooking up and disappearing two by two.

"My eyes were opening and closing intermittently; at one point, I opened my eyes and this Asian girl was sitting next to me. I would talk to her a little bit, pass out for a while, and then she would say something else and I'd open my eyes again. I really tried to maintain a conversation with her. I also thought that she was playing with me at one point because I'd be talking to her and she'd be sitting on my right side. Then I'd close my eyes and the next thing I knew, I was talking to her on my left side. I remember wondering if she was taking advantage of me or just messing with me psychologically, and thinking, *What the fuck is going on here? Why is she constantly switching sides?*"

"That does sound confusing. What were the two of you talking about? Did you talk about sex?" Kelli asked, trying to sound professional.

Jake winked at her. "Do you want to hear about our sex talk, Kelli?" He leaned forward. She could smell him again.

"Well, uh, yes. If it's relevant." She felt shy.

"Oh," Jake laughed and sat back again, "I see. 'If it's relevant.' Well, I'll try to keep it very relevant for you." He smirked a little. She ignored it and he continued.

"Well the first thing I remember, the girl on the right was actually asking me a question. She was flirting, and I remember her leaning in and asking me, 'Have you ever been with an Asian woman?' I said, 'Yes, actually. I was with an Asian girl at my senior prom.'

"'Oh? Did you like it?' asked the girl sitting next to me. Only this time she was sitting on my left, which was very confusing in my drunken state.

"'It's a complicated story,' I answered. I wasn't in any shape to tell the whole story to her right then and there. I think I passed out shortly afterward.

"I came to when the girl on my right asked, 'Do you want to be with an Asian girl again?'

"I must have answered yes because then the girl on the left was asking me, 'Do you like threesomes?' This confused me even more. Who would the threesome be with?"

Kelli laughed. "I can tell there is some kind of twist here. I bet it's about to get interesting." Jake smiled back at her and nodded.

"Yes, there's a twist. Towards the end of the night, I woke up and was stretched out on the couch. Both of my hands were being held. I realized that one of my hands was being held by the Asian woman I'd been talking to all night, and the other was held by a second woman who happened to look exactly like the first. It turned out that they were identical twins! Later, I realized that both sisters had been talking to me at various times, one on the left and one on the right, and I had been too drunk and unaware to realize it."

"Wow. Twins. That's crazy," commented Kelli. "What on Earth happened?"

"The sisters gently pulled me up off of the couch and before I knew what was going on, they led me to the door of an empty bedroom. They asked me if I had ever been with two women before, and specifically if I had ever been with twins. I told them no, I hadn't, and that in fact I had very little sexual experience in general. They seemed pleased enough by this confession, and started to kiss and undress me. One pulled my shirt over my head and started flicking my nipples with her tongue, while the other one started gently massaging my groin area and balls. I can remember thinking, *Wow. I can't believe that my first ever threesome is going to be with twins.* I was struggling to get my boots off, and finally one boot slipped off and flew across the room. The force knocked me backwards onto the bed, where I passed out.

"The next thing I remember was waking up, lying in the bed naked with the twins next to me, one on each side, dozing. As I started to stir, they also began to wake up. I asked them what had happened and they both laughed and told me that absolutely nothing had happened. I had passed out and that was the end of it. I couldn't believe it, and felt like an idiot, but they just laughed it off. I was eager to make it up to them and asked them for their number, but they wouldn't give it out. They said they were looking for someone who could really perform, and it was obvious that I couldn't hold my liquor or perform. So that ended that."

"What did you do then?" asked Kelli. "Were you embarrassed?"

"Yes, a little. It was morning already, and feeling like an ass, I got dressed and walked out into the living room. It was somewhat trashed after the party, of course. The girl that I had noticed the night before—the beautiful, voluptuous Latina—was picking up trash and putting it into a garbage bag. She smiled at me, and in that moment I met a woman who changed my life. She stuck out her hand and introduced herself. Her name was Marci Lopez, and I found out later that she was Puerto Rican.

"In any case, she looked me over and giggled knowingly, with those bright, dark, almond-shaped eyes twinkling. There was a beautiful sincerity in her gaze, a compassionate, almost loving aspect. Then she nodded towards the bedroom, where the Korean twins were getting dressed and said, 'You really haven't been with too many women, have you?'

"I sat down; hung my aching, pounding head and said, 'No. Not really.'

"Marci set down her trash bag and sat next to me on the couch. She took my hand and said, 'Listen. You're adorable, and this is what is going to happen from now on: You are going to come over to my house on a regular basis. We're not going to actually do anything; you need to just learn how to kiss and how to talk to a woman. I'm going to teach you!' I was amazed.

"'Um, why would you do that?' I asked her.

"She giggled, and I could not help but notice her beautiful, intense eyes again. 'Well, I'm almost done with college, and I'm super busy with my classes and studies. I don't really have the time for a serious, full-time boyfriend, but I do have needs and I think you're cute. You need a teacher, and I need a good fuck once in a while with someone who is clean, trustworthy, and a good friend. Also, you sound like you could carry on a decent conversation. I like smart guys. How does that sound?'

"I couldn't really believe my luck; before I knew it, I was on my way back to my dorm with her number in my pocket."

Kelli interrupted him, "Did you call her?"

Jake gazed intently at her. "Yes, Kelli. I called her. And then, I fucked her."

Kelli flinched slightly at the abrupt choice of words. "You fucked her?"

"Yeah. I fucked her a lot. You want to hear about it, don't you?" It was a serious question. He looked into her eyes and she could feel herself wanting, needing more. She needed to hear about his sexual past.

"Go on," she breathed.

"Over the course of three months or so, Marci gave me a true education. In between classes, whenever I had two or three hours to spare, I would ride my bike over to Marci's and she would be there. At first, she would draw me into her bedroom and strip me down to my underwear. She'd take off her shirt, under which she'd be braless, and then she would push me down and lie on top of me in bed.

"At first I was shy, and she would take my hand and run it all over her body. I soon learned how to massage her full, heavy breasts, and how to tweak her large nipples gently between my finger and thumb. We'd make out for hours. She taught me how to kiss, how to use my tongue, how to caress, how to nibble and bite her mouth and neck, and how to touch her in a way that made her moan with pleasure. I loved that more than anything else—learning how to really make Marci moan. She especially loved the light biting; there was one incident where Marci actually bit my shoulder hard enough to leave a small bruise. She told me it was her way of marking me.

"One day, after a few weeks of heavy petting, Marci took things a step further. We'd been kissing for a while and then she took my hand and guided it down between her legs. She'd never done that before; everything had been pretty much above the waist, except for some mild grinding and dry humping. She was naked except for boy-short panties, and she guided my fingers down between the cloth and her hot, soft skin. I felt the wiriness of her pubic hair—she kept a tidy little landing strip—and then felt, for the first time, the incredible, slick wetness of her pussy. Marci took my middle finger and slid it inside of her, moaning a little, and offering up her neck for me to kiss. Then she took two fingers of mine, the middle and the forefinger; pushed them up inside her tight, warm pussy; and rocked herself back and forth on my hand.

"It wasn't enough. After a while, her movements became almost frantic and she tore off her panties completely, and placed her palm on the top of my head and pushed me down, in between her firm, shapely legs. I was dizzy with excitement. Elaine had gone down on me, that day long ago when I lost my virginity, but I had never tasted a woman before this. The scent of Marci's pussy was sweet and heavy. She told me to run my tongue lightly over the wide open lips of her pussy and I obeyed. The slick, tangy taste of her was intoxicating. She spread her knees wider and drew her own hand down to the top of her cleft, where her clit was pink, glistening, and protruding. 'Touch me here with your tongue, Jake,' she whispered, massaging it lightly with her fingertips. Again, I obeyed; flicking her with my tongue, and the resulting sound that came out of her, was incredible.

"'Again. Softer. Lick around it. Gently.' I followed her detailed instructions as she ordered me to suck and caress her throbbing, firm, and swollen bud of flesh. That day, I ate her out for the first time, probing, licking, and kissing. Occasionally, she would order me to pause for a minute and come up and kiss her for a while before pushing my head back down to her pussy. Eventually, she arched her back and thrust her soft, wet flesh onto my tongue as I probed her. She climaxed incredibly hard, screaming and moaning. The amount of wet fluid that gushed out with her orgasm was amazing to me. I drank it, lapping it with my tongue. Marci had taught me one awesome trick, something I do to this very day."

Kelli quickly shouted, "What? Tell me!!"

"Marci had pointed out to me that at the point of orgasm for women, the clit becomes enlarged, and points out. She demanded that I suck her clit hard and pull it inside my mouth as hard as possible as she came, my mouth cupping her hood and my tongue licking at the same time that I pulled her clit hard during her orgasm. Something all women I've been with love, and tell me I'm the best at doing."

"Oh, wow," Kelli sighed.

"Going down on Marci became a regular part of our routine together. One day, she had another surprise in store for me. When I came into her bedroom, she was naked, and next to her on the bed was a gigantic vibrator, the same type that was made famous by a popular TV show. You know the one…the Rabbit."

Kelli smiled. She'd heard of the Rabbit. "Yes, I know the one," she said.

I must have looked shocked or bewildered because Marci giggled and beckoned me over to her. 'I want to teach you how to use a toy today,' she said, those black eyes twinkling.

"I lay down beside her and she turned on the vibrator. First, she used it on herself, dipping it into her wet pussy over and over again, pushing the vibrating 'ears' against her clit until she came hard and fast, shrieking with pleasure. I had never seen her convulse and tremble so much. Then she put it into my hand. 'Your turn to fuck me now,' she said teasingly.

"She guided me as I first ran the vibrating tip along the firm mound of her stomach, and touched it to her nipples, making them hard. She made me tease her and turn her on like this for a while, touching her thighs, her stomach, and her breasts. She loved the sensation of it buzzing against her skin. Finally, she wrapped her hand around mine and spread her thighs wide, drawing the toy all the way deep inside her juicy pussy. 'Like this. Feel the rhythm of it.'

"I moved my hand with hers, and saw and felt her get wetter and wetter as it slipped in and out, going deeper and deeper. She arched her back and drew it in even further. When I got a little excited and started thrusting too fast, Marci slowed me down, teaching me the rhythm. She came three, four, five times that way.

"Playing with toys became a regular thing, just as eating her out had become normal. Of course, doing these things to her also aroused me to a fever pitch, and Marci wasn't cruel; she would eventually allow me to cum after she herself had climaxed multiple times. She never let me actually cum inside her, but she would give me a hand job, or blowjob, and let me cum all over her breasts, stomach, and thighs.

"Another day, Marci pulled out a length of silken rope from a drawer next to her bed. 'I want to tie you up,' she whispered, as she straddled me. Her actions reminded me of the incident with Elaine in high school. Those memories were not necessarily all positive, and Marci must have seen the uncertainty in my face.

"'I'll be gentle, Jake,' she said. 'Why don't we use a safe word?'

"I had never heard of a 'safe word' before. 'What is that?'

"'Well, we choose a word. For instance, one that I like to use is *Georgia*. In our sex play, if either one of us says the word *Georgia*, that means that things are going too far and we need to dial it back. So if I tie you up, as long as you are enjoying yourself, we both go along with the role play. But if you become uncomfortable, say, 'Georgia,' and I'll know that you really mean it. Does that work for you?'

"I nodded, and Marci proceeded to tie me up. The experience was actually incredible this time around. She had lit some candles in her room and the flickering light created amazing shadows on the wall. Marci placed a blindfold over my eyes, and left me bound on the bed while she went to the kitchen. I wasn't sure what she was doing, but heard the fridge open, and then the clattering sound of the ice box. When she came back, she touched me and had something in her hand.

"'Just lie back and enjoy,' she murmured.

"Then I felt the most extraordinary sensation. She was rubbing an ice cube over my chest and abs. She traced the ice all around my torso, down my thighs, and then down into my groin region. My cock was completely rigid. She rubbed the ice cube around my shaft and I moaned a little. Then the ice cube was gone and Marci was tracing the path of the cold water with her warm tongue. The combination of cold and warm was completely exhilarating.

"When she reached my cock with her mouth, she sucked me long and hard. Just when I was close to cumming, she climbed on top of me and started to ride me. This was her favorite position; it allowed her to grind her clit against me and she often came multiple times. This occasion was no different, and ended in her having her way with me as she gushed orgasmic fluids all over my dick. After she came, she slipped off of me and took me in her mouth. The feeling of her lips around me caused me to climax hard. I couldn't help myself and shouted out, 'Elaine!'

Kelli was shocked. "You said another girl's name during sex? How did Marci react?"

Jake chuckled. "She stopped…and then she reached up and slapped my face."

"Slapped your face? Wow. I guess I'm not really surprised."

"Yes. And then she got ahold of herself and asked me why I had just done that. I told her that the girl to whom I'd lost my virginity was named Elaine, and my sex with Marci had brought back those memories. I told her a little bit about the situation and what it had done to me. Marci was angry, but she had a compassionate heart and she forgave me. She was just like that."

Kelli was wild with curiosity, and wasn't sure if her voice was steady, but said, "Sounds…like an incredible interaction." Jake just nodded and continued.

"In any case, overall, Marci taught me how to treat a woman sexually. Our sexual sessions went on all the way to the end of my freshman year, which was also the end of her junior year. At that time, she told me, 'Jake, this has been great fun, but next year I really have to focus on my schoolwork because I'm transferring to California. But try to remember and use everything I've taught you, and try to find a really good woman for yourself and get some good experience. You're going to need it because when you do decide to settle down and marry, your wife is going to want you to be very good in bed.' We parted as friends, and I took her advice to heart. It was a while before I had the chance to practice all that she had taught me, but it was extremely useful in the end.

"Marci taught me the foundations of what I know today. I have to give her credit; she holds a significant role in my adventures, as a warm and affectionate woman who was phenomenally creative, in the sexual sense, and who took the time to educate me in the mysteries of the female body. Whenever a lover comments on my oral skills or my sexual creativity, I think of Marci and all she taught me."

Kelli was squirming in her chair, and hoping that Jake wouldn't notice how much his story had aroused her. "Wow. That's amazing to have had such an affectionate and thorough teacher. So what else happened during your time in Boston?"

"Well, during my college senior year, I was called home because my father was diagnosed with terminal cancer at a late stage. So I wasn't actually able to finish out my senior year. I was offered a job that had a very lucrative salary, so I decided to go to night school, and I moved back to my hometown to spend time with my dying father."

Kelli heard the note of tenderness and sadness in Jake's voice, and was moved. Was that moistness in his eyes as he spoke of his father? She believed it was. So this tough, dominant man had a soft side too, it appeared. She thought it might be best to steer away from such sensitive ground.

"So, then did you ever have a meaningful serious relationship with a woman? As in, a real girlfriend?" A huge part of her wanted to hear about more of his sexual experiences. However, another, tenderer part was interested in the emotional side. What had he learned? What had he felt?

"Yes. I became involved with this one girl sorta recently, HazelEyed Vixen."

Jake's voice trailed off. Kelli was surprised. She had never seen him have such a dreamy, sad look.

"You don't have to talk about it, you know," she said. "If you'd rather not, I mean."

Jake looked at her and said, "No, no. It's fine. She messaged me recently, back when I went to Vegas after you and I first met, and it's been complicated since.

"Things were just intense with V, that's all. I'll tell you a story. It had been a long, hard, and stressful day at work. It was 4:30 p.m. when I got her text. It read, '520 {v}.' I knew, and she knew, that we both needed it. The '520' represented the date we first felt each other, a special meaning to me, and the lowercase *v* in brackets was the sign of her submissiveness to me, being collared. It was a long drive home, the winter had been cold and icy, the worst in years. I pulled into the driveway of my house, and watched the melting ice start to freeze over the house as the temperature dropped again. I looked over the dripping water on my rain gutter, observing the water freezing into jagged ice as the temperature dropped lower and lower. This gave me an idea. I broke off a newly-formed icy point from the chain of icicles. I knew I was going to tease her with the cold, torturous object. Walking to the house, I got another text: 'Sir 520 {v} I await you.'

"I walked into the house and there was my angel, my HazelEyed Vixen, on her knees in the submissive position, waiting for me. I grabbed her hand and walked her to my sitting chair. Slowly, I bent her over my lap and proceeded to tell her about my frustrating day. Between sentences, I gave her several firm spanks on one ass cheek, holding her flesh, feeling the rush of blood running through her body. I spanked her other cheek also, as not to neglect it, and felt the rush of sexuality running through my veins.

"I told her, 'Angel, today is your day.' Walking her to the bedroom, I blindfolded her and strapped her wrists to each bedpost. The icicle was still on a platter in the front room, still hard and thick. I brought it to the bedroom, took the icicle, and began tracing her body. I worked the icicle from her left hand, wrist, arm, and shoulder over to her ear, cheeks, mouth, and lips. I slowly made my way down to her left nipple, the bottom of her chest, down her stomach, across her pubic bone, around her thighs and back up her right side, slowly making my way to her right wrist. By now, the icicle was half melted from her body heat, and my angel was worming and squirming on the bed; I retraced the same path slowly with the tip of my tongue, kissing her mouth, biting her lips, stopping at her nipple for a hard bite, teasing her fiery pussy with my mouth, and back up to her right nipple and wrist. She was holding back her orgasm and I told her that today she would cum hard.

"Keeping her bound, I worked my way down her body with my mouth, water glistening off her hot skin, till I made my way to her already throbbing clit. Holding her legs down with my arms, I tasted her sweet juices, sucked hard on her pussy lips and clit, and kissed the hood passionately. I told her to release; I wanted to taste her juices. She came hard as I sucked and pulled her clit into my mouth. As I held her legs, she tried to buck free. I crawled my way back up her shivering body, as she begged me to be inside her, and I teased her clit and hood with the tip of my mushroom cock. I leaned in and whispered into her ear, 'Angel, I want to feel you in my own way: *scissors*.' She nodded her head; she knew what I wanted.

"I released her hands from the bedposts and moved her to her right side. I straddled her right leg, and lifted her left leg bent onto a pillow. I had a full view of her amazing ass and pussy that was throbbing and calling for my cock to go deep inside her. I took the half melted icicle and slowly placed it inside her, as she moaned with extreme pleasure. I pulled it out, tasted her amazing juices, and then I plunged my already hard cock deep inside her, legs interlocked. I lifted her left ass cheek a bit more so I could get deeper. I took her hard and furious, releasing my day's frustrations out on her. Banging furiously and forcefully, I told her I needed her to taste my release.

"I wanted to see her beautiful eyes gazing at me as she took in all of me. She felt me getting bigger and harder as I wet my thumb slowly and began teasing her cute asshole, penetrating it gently. She couldn't take the thumb anal probe and my thick cock simultaneously bumping her g-spot. It was amazingly tight, and she came again in rippling fashion; she couldn't stop pushing herself deeper onto my shaft. I watched her pussy lips hug my shaft with each in-and-out thrust. I needed to cum now, and I told her it was time.

"She jumped off, and I grabbed the blindfold off of her and pushed hard into her waiting mouth. I watched her viciously suck my member, enjoying it and trying to get every sweet drop of cum out of me. Watching her amazingly beautiful eyes tear up, I exploded in her hot mouth as she swirled her tongue around the back edge of my tip, just how I liked it. I grabbed the back of her head and held her there, *OMG! Amazing!* She knew to keep sucking and taking every drop. She also knew we could go again, but not today. Now I just wanted to hold her close, treasuring what I had found."

Jake's voice trailed off. He had a faraway look in his eye.

Kelli was blown away. She couldn't even imagine the sexual intensity that Jake had just described to her. It had turned her on in a big way. She was squirming just imagining what it would be like to be in the place of the HazelEyed Vixen. She could barely concentrate on keeping it together. She was wondering what to say or do next, when she glanced at her watch and was shocked to see that the time was 6:05 p.m. The hour was up.

"Oh, um, yes. We'd better stop for today. We'll continue next time."

She fumbled with her legal pad and then realized that Jake had moved closer, and was now standing right next to her. She could smell his cologne, and it made her dizzy.

As if Jake could read her mind or sense what she was thinking about, he spoke. His tone was soft, but firm.

"Kelli, I can smell your perfume very strongly. Too strongly, in fact. It's overpowering and I don't like it."

Kelli felt ashamed and looked at the floor. She had been so conscious about choosing a scent that morning; she had wanted to smell nice for him. Had wanted to please him. But he was unhappy; he was displeased with her efforts.

Jake stretched out his hand and drew her chin up so that she was looking into his striking green eyes.

"I don't mind your choice of scent, but don't wear so much of it. Not tomorrow, or the next day, or next Monday at our appointment. Not any day. Do I make myself clear, Kelli?"

Intensely conscious of his fingers on her cheek, Kelli nodded. "Yes, I understand."

Jake released her gently and took a step back. "Good. Very good. Because if you disobey, I will be very, very displeased." He smiled that dazzling smile and Kelli felt a part of herself melt.

"Until next time, then." Jake turned and started towards the door. When he reached it, he stood with his hand on the doorknob and paused, as if forgetting something. He looked back at her. "Oh, and Kelli? There is one more thing."

"Yes?"

"I want you to go buy yourself some new toys. Like the toys that Marci had. There's a shop called Secret Closet that isn't too far from here. Stop in on your way home and buy at least one. Will you do that?" His gaze was commanding and irresistible.

"Um…uh…yes. OK." Kelli could feel her cheeks flushing hot and bright red.

Jake nodded approvingly. "Good girl." Then he was gone.

Kelli left work and got into a cab. She was about to give the cab driver her home address when she suddenly changed her mind. "Secret Closet, please," she told him instead.

The Secret Closet was only ten or eleven blocks away, but traffic was slow and sticky, so Kelli let her head rest against the back of the seat and quickly became lost in thought.

Part of her, the part that had wanted to go straight home, was annoyed with Jake. Annoyed because he was so damn bossy. *Who does he think he is?* she asked herself. *And I already have vibrators at home, anyway. What does he think I am, some sex-starved, needy nympho?* Then she found herself wincing internally, because really, *wasn't* she sex-starved and needy? Who was she kidding? Yes, she did have vibrators at home but they were fairly pathetic. One was a little vibrating tube shaped like a lipstick that she'd won as a door prize at a bachelorette party a few years ago. She'd never even used it. The other one…she did use, but it was just a little egg-shaped bullet. She used it from time to time, and it did the trick well enough, but she knew that there were better toys out there.

She had always felt self-conscious about having them at all. What if Paul found them in her underwear drawer or on the side of the bathtub? She used to care, but now, with Jake's cologne still in her nose and the feeling of his fingers burning on her cheeks, she realized that she didn't care at all about Paul finding a vibrator. *Let him find twenty! What difference does it make? None.* She was ready to take control.

In any case, it's not like using a vibrator was cheating, so why should she care what Paul thought? Paul already knew that she got herself off from time to time; he'd even walked in on her before. So now was the time to really let loose. About Jake being too bossy…well, another part of her didn't seem to mind it one bit. Why else did she obey him so readily? *Because I want to. That's why.*

She had made up her mind on what to buy before she even entered the store. She marched straight up to the clerk and said, "I would like to buy your best-selling vibrator. You know the one I mean. The famous one, with the little vibrating 'ears.'"

The clerk looked at her with a bored expression, snapped her gum, and said, "Uh huh. The Rabbits are over here." She walked Kelli past a shelf full of XXX videos and a rack of racy thigh-highs and suspenders, then pointed to a huge cabinet full of dildos and vibrators. The model that Kelli wanted was prominently displayed and available in five colors. Kelli chose red. Glancing around the shop, she felt incredibly alive and sexy. She spotted a pair of fuzzy white handcuffs and on a whim picked them up as well. *Why not? A girl can dream.* She took the handcuffs and the vibrator to the front and paid the bored clerk, who wrapped up her purchases in a nondescript paper bag.

Kelli arrived home to find the apartment dark and empty. *Oh, right,* she thought. *Monday night football.* With a certain amount of glee, she realized that Paul would be gone for at least another two hours, if not more. *He'll probably be drinking,* she realized, and for the first time in years, that thought made her smile.

She considered dinner, but realized that she wasn't at all hungry. Not for food anyway. She knew exactly what she wanted.

She walked to the master bathroom, and with a growing sense of anticipation, began to draw a bath into the huge whirlpool bathtub. She collected some tea lights from a bedroom drawer, lit them around her bathroom strategically, and poured some scented bath salts into the steaming water. Dimming the lights so that the candlelight flickered and cast patterns on the walls, she carefully unwrapped her new toy. Feeling grateful for its waterproof properties, she set it to the side on the bath tiles.

Then she slowly stripped naked, removing each piece of clothing inch by inch, and stepped slowly and deliberately into the bath water. She felt her muscles relax and unwind, and as they did, she also felt raw, primal desire take hold of her body, running lines of fire up between her legs. Her sexual need was suddenly intense and overwhelming. *My god, Jake is so fucking sexy*, she thought, running her hands through the water. *This has never happened with a client before. Not like this. I want to fuck him. To be fucked by him. Christ, how I want to be fucked by him.*

With this thought in her mind, she picked up the vibrator and turned it on, hoisting her hips up slightly so that the warm water lapped at the sides like a tongue. Her pussy was exposed and ready to be penetrated; the thick, nine-inch vibrator slipped inside of her effortlessly, gyrating, throbbing, and massaging her sweet spot. Kelli moved it in and out of her aching lips and the slick patch between her legs, her breath coming faster and faster. The feeling of the firm, solid rubber dildo filling up her pussy, pushing against the walls of her flesh, was satisfying beyond belief. She could feel the top of it tickling and stimulating her hard, swollen clit, sending waves of pleasure throughout her whole body.

She thought of Jake sitting in her office. *Jake, in his designer suits, with his green, green eyes, his cologne, his incredible smile, his hand touching her face. The smell of his skin and his commanding presence telling her to obey. Then naked, his bare chest, her hands bound in the fuzzy white cuffs, and his hard cock thrusting inside her, and...and...*within just a few short minutes, she felt the ultimate wave of her climax crash over and through her, and her whole body spasmed hard, arching upward, her thighs clenching helplessly around the still-buzzing vibrator as she came and came, convulsing helplessly eight, ten, twelve times.

That was just the beginning. Paul wouldn't be home for a long time. Kelli's body was limp against the warm, slippery porcelain of the bathtub and the vibrator was silent. She rested there, for just a moment…then flipped the switch back on and started again.

{ 5 }

Over the remainder of the week and into the weekend, Kelli couldn't stop using her new toy, the Rabbit vibrator, and she couldn't stop thinking about Jake and the story he had told her about his encounters with Marci Lopez. She felt restless and horny, so much so that she almost considered approaching Paul and trying—for the thousandth time—to initiate sex. She thought better of that idea, however, and found herself dialing Nina's number instead.

"Kelli, babe. What's up? Are you fucking that client of yours yet?"

"God, Nina. You are so amazingly crude sometimes. NO, I'm not fucking him."

"You're crazy, girl! That's some hot shit right there!"

"Yeah, well there is this little thing called professionalism. Ever heard of it?"

"Whatever. You know you want him. So, what's going on, for real?"

"Well, I actually…I was thinking…want to go out again? Maybe tonight?"

"Of course I do. Actually, I was already planning to hit up the XXXXX club. A few other girls are going to be there, too. Kind of a ladies' night out. Want to join?"

Kelli did want to join, very much. The two made plans to meet and Kelli spent the rest of Saturday afternoon figuring out what to wear. She remembered Jake's description of Marci and her curves, and she felt inspired to show off her own assets. Men had always lusted after her shapely ass and mile-high legs, which were complemented by her willowy waist. She often wore skirts and heels to show off her legs and butt, but she decided that tonight called for something special.

She combed through the selections in her wardrobe and finally pulled out a slinky, deep royal purple dress. She hadn't worn it in a while; the plunging *V*-shaped neckline and asymmetrical cut of the hem were slightly on the racy side, yet managed to be elegant rather than trashy. She removed it from its garment bag and held it up to herself in the mirror. *Yes, this should do.* It would look perfect if she pulled her hair up into a long, tousled ponytail and completed the ensemble with some gorgeous dangly gold earrings. *Not too bad,* she thought as she looked at herself. *Not bad at all.*

That night, the club was heaving. As was often the case, Nina knew the owner of the club and was able to secure a table in the VIP section for Kelli, Nina, and the other women who had joined them. As Kelli sipped her dirty martini and sucked the bleu cheese out of her olives one by one, she surveyed the bar and had flashbacks to the time that she had first laid eyes on Jake. She felt herself get a little wet just thinking about the calm, confident way that he had stared her down, and his dominant manner during their sessions. The chatter of the women around her didn't even sink in as she thought back to the stories that Jake had told her. *He must be such an amazing lover.*

Kelli felt herself becoming even more swollen and aroused at the thought. She squirmed and crossed her legs. As she did so, she saw several men staring at her lustfully. *Yeah,* she thought to herself. *You just keep on looking.* She suddenly had an almost uncontrollable urge to part her legs and give them a look at how she had gone commando under her dress, Sharon Stone style. But she thought better of it. Somehow, she sensed that Jake wouldn't want her to cheapen herself like that, no matter how sexual she felt. The thought of his disapproval was sobering. She demurely avoided making direct eye contact with the various men who were checking her out, and soon after excused herself to Nina.

"Nina, thanks so much for inviting me out, but I'm going to take off now."

Nina was shocked that Kelli was already leaving.

"Girl, what is with you? The night is young, and unless you've gone blind, I'm sure you've seen the guys who have been drooling over you. What happened to having some fun?"

Kelli winced. "I do want to have fun, Nina. I'm just…just not in the mood. I'm going to head out."

Nina shrugged. "Have it your way, sweetheart. See you soon!"

Later, Kelli slipped into the bathtub and turned on her Rabbit. Thinking of Jake, she brought herself to climax four times before she finally felt like she could sleep. As she climbed between her satin sheets and tried to shut out the monotonous drone of Paul's heavy snoring, she had only one thought echoing through her mind and her body: *Monday, Monday, Monday…*

The next day was Sunday and it seemed to take a million years to go by. After what seemed like an interminable amount of time, Monday finally arrived. In the morning, as she prepared to go to the office, Kelli was very careful not to apply her usual amount of perfume as per Jake's request. Instead, she dabbed just the faintest amount on her wrists and behind her ears; just enough to have a slight waft of scent about her.

When he arrived for his appointment, she was sitting, waiting for him. She had left him the big therapist's chair, the one that he always chose. As he entered the room, she looked up and smiled at him. Jake returned her smile, and without saying a word, brought his face close to hers and sniffed her. His smile got bigger.

"Good girl, Kelli. Good girl. I can smell your perfume, but you obeyed me. You are very obedient. I like that."

He sat in front of her, arms spread across the back of the chair with one leg crossed over the other. Again, Kelli noted his body language: confident, strong, and calm.

She spoke, "So, judging from the stories you told me last time about Marci and the threesome, you must have really played around with women."

Jake grinned. "Sure. As it happens, I had a pretty intense encounter within the last week or so. You wouldn't believe it if I told you."

Kelli smiled. "Try me!"

"OK. So last week, a woman told me at the bar that she wanted to fuck me, and something clicked in my mind. I remembered what had happened between us prior, even if she didn't. She and I had a history together, but she was clearly clueless about it.

"With that in mind, I slipped her one of my business cards while her friend was busy putting on her coat. I didn't say a word to the first woman, just smiled at her calmly. *That should do the trick*, I thought to myself.

"I said goodbye to both women and told the second one that I would see her very soon.

"Driving home, my mind kept returning to the second woman. I liked her a lot more than the first, but soon thoughts of the first one overtook me.

"It had all happened two years ago, as I was just embarking on my journey of transformation. At the time, I was still significantly overweight and out of shape. It had reached the point where it was profoundly affecting my interactions with women. I had joined the affair site and had been a member for only a few weeks when I spotted this woman. She was sexy and flirty, and responded quickly to my messages, so we arranged to meet for dinner. I told her that I loved sushi, and she said she did too. As it happened, there was a great little sushi place, Sushi Yamu, close to where we both lived, so we arranged to meet there.

"When she came in, I stood up to greet her and instantly knew that things were not going to go well. She looked me up and down and didn't even try to hide her reaction. Clearly, I was not what she was expecting. She sat down abruptly, took up a menu, ordered, and ate as quickly as possible. I tried to mask my disappointment; we definitely had a connection online and I had hoped that it would continue in person.

"The meal was short and awkward. At the end, I offered to walk her to her car, and she turned to me and said something that stuck with me for a long, long time: 'Look, Jake. You're nice and everything, but I just don't think that there is a romantic future for us, OK? You're just...not my type. Maybe if you worked out a little bit more we might have a chance, but....' Her sentence trailed off as she looked at me and just shook her head, her full lips in a disapproving pout. I was in shock; I couldn't believe how rude she was being.

"'Uh, OK,' I blurted out. And with that, she walked away.

"Her words had really stung, and I had fantasized many times about what I'd like to do and say to her if our paths ever crossed again. I thought of fucking her, fast and furious...driving my cock into her wet pussy while she begged for more and more. Now, against all the odds, here she was...offering to fuck me! *This is too crazy*, I thought.

"Not even a few days later, my phone buzzed and I saw that I had a text message. Crazily, the name was Sushi Woman. I couldn't believe it, but apparently her number was still saved in my phone from two years earlier. The text read:

"'Hey sexy. It's me, from Dolce Vita. Wanna grab a bite sometime this week? Xoxoxoxoxo'"

"*Dolce Vita?* The SAME place where we met?" Kelli interrupted.

"Yes. Weird, right?" Jake chuckled.

"Anyway, I didn't reply right away. Not for two full days. *Let her really, really want it,* I thought. Finally, I responded brusquely: 'OK. Sushi Yamu, tomorrow. 7:30 p.m.' That was it. I wondered if the name of the sushi joint would spark her memory.

"She answered my text within twenty minutes. 'OK, see you there hot stuff! Xoxoxoxoxo.'

"Clearly, she hadn't made the connection.

"I couldn't believe how easy this was. What a shallow bitch! Obviously, she was only interested in the slim, ripped Jake. I found myself fantasizing again about what I would do to her if I got her into bed...I was going to take out my frustrations on her, show her who was boss. I imagined her face contorting as I thrust my swollen cock in and out of her mouth, and how her thighs would quiver with anticipation as I made her hold back from cumming. Oh yes, she was about to see a new me.

"In contrast to our first date two years ago, she arrived on time to Sushi Yamu. I, however, did not. I deliberately kept her waiting for a solid twenty minutes before strolling in without apology.

"She was sitting at a little corner table and sprang up immediately. 'Oh, hi, Jake!' she said, smiling widely and far too eagerly. She was wearing a tiny little red sparkly mini dress made of stretchy material that clung to every curve, along with some platform stilettos. Almost nothing about her figure was left to the imagination. I had to admit, she did have a smoking hot body. Looking at her large, luscious breasts popping out of her dress, I felt my cock stiffen a little in anticipation of what I was going to do to her. But I couldn't forget the way that she had treated me in the past. She would feel the sting of my anger before the night was over.

"We ordered food, and she proceeded to flirt outrageously, telling suggestive sexual jokes and running her hand over my arm whenever she had the chance. The waiter came and took our order: four pieces of sashimi salmon, two pieces of sashimi tuna, and two double shots of cold sake. I told him we were probably going to be in a hurry, and asked if he could rush the order. The food and drinks came almost immediately, as I was a regular there. I knew she loved the raw meat, as did I, and we pounded down the sake quickly. About half an hour into the meal, I noticed that she had slipped off one of her heels and was rubbing her bare foot up and down my calf. I simply moved my leg and pretended not to notice.

"I could tell that the cold shoulder treatment was really getting to her; she started to become more and more desperate as we finished and I called for the bill.

"'Jake...I really have to tell you something,' she said. She leaned forward, her black curls brushing her face and her cleavage opening up almost down to her navel.

"'Oh, what is it?' I leaned back with my arm stretched casually along the chair next to me.

"'Well, I probably shouldn't say this, but ever since I saw you in the bar...I, well, I just haven't wanted to fuck a guy so badly in months. Years, maybe. I just thought you should know.'

"I kept my face passive, staring firmly but happily into her eyes. 'Oh? Huh. That's interesting. What makes me so fuckable, then?' I asked, knowing how shallow she really was.

"She giggled. 'I'm not even sure. I mean, it could be your face and body. You are definitely hot. But I think it's more of how you carry yourself. You're so damn confident! It just makes me want to slide my hands inside your pants to see what I'll find, honestly.'

"'Hmmm. Well, do you want to get out of here?' I realized that it was time for her schooling to begin.

"'Hell, yeah!'

"We went outside and she practically threw herself into my arms once we hit the parking lot. I led her over to my car and pressed her up against it, holding her wrists tightly above her head in one hand while I ran the other up and down her body, kneading and massaging her curves. She began moaning loudly and squirming against me. I thrust my hand up inside her mini dress and as I expected, she wasn't wearing any panties. She was clean shaven and already soaking wet.

"While still holding her wrists in one hand, I immediately put three fingers of the other hand deep inside her dripping pussy and then slowly finger-fucked her for just a minute or two, enough to make her moan louder, gasp, and start quivering slightly. When she started to buck against my hand, I pulled my fingers out very slowly and deliberately, and, while keeping constant eye contact, I put them in my mouth and sucked off her juices. She tasted hot and ready. Then I pushed the same fingers in her mouth and she sucked off the remnants of her own pussy juice. The feeling of her mouth sucking my fingers made my cock throb. I would need to fuck her soon.

"She was so excited by this that she could barely talk, but she managed to gasp, 'Where are you going to take me?'

"I laughed and reached into her dress to pinch one of her nipples. She had enormous nipples, round and firm like cherries.

"'Oh, I'm not taking you anywhere. I'm going to have my way with you right here. Now get in the back of the car.'

"With those words, I opened the car door and then gently yet firmly pushed her head down so that she entered the car. I could see her firm, luscious ass, bare and round, sticking out towards me temptingly with her dress hiked up around her waist. I slapped each cheek lightly while standing behind her, and she let out a gasp of pleasure. Then I gripped both ass cheeks in my hands and pried them open, just a little, to see her little, round asshole. I leaned forward and ran my tongue down over her protruding labia, sucking up some of her juices. I stuck my tongue deep in her pussy and then worked my way up to flick her ass ever so slightly. She was moaning now, fast and furiously.

"I wasn't about to let her have her pleasure, though. Mine would come first. I slid into the back seat beside her and undid my zipper, pulling out my swollen manhood. Grabbing her hair in my hand I pushed her trembling mouth down towards my crotch.

"'Suck me off, woman,' I told her authoritatively. She needed to know who was in charge. Her lips closed around my huge, throbbing cock eagerly. I'd never seen a woman who wanted to blow me so much. She was very skilled at what she did, massaging my balls while she pulled the whole of my shaft deep down into her throat. She alternated her deep-throating action, taking my balls into her mouth, licking and sucking them, while working and stroking my fat cock with one hand. She was good. Very good.

"I knew that if she kept blowing me I'd come too soon, so I changed it up a little.

"'You're going to ride me now,' I breathed into her ear, biting her lobe a little after I spoke. 'You're going to ride me like a little bitch.'

"She was flushed and totally losing control. She just nodded mutely. I ripped her bra off one shoulder and she took my cue, loosening the hooks in the back. It fell away and I saw her huge, fleshy breasts bouncing in the faint light from the streetlamps. I cradled one in each hand and lifted my head up to suck and bite her nipple again.

"Then I pulled her on top of me, and she let out a huge gasp as she felt the whole of my cock enter her soaking wet pussy, filling her up. She stayed still for just a brief moment, feeling me. Then she started to rock, moaning like a wild animal while she did so.

"I knew that I needed to cum before she did because I had plans for her. Rather than hold back, I let her pussy clench around me and I knew I was going to cum soon.

"I grabbed her hair again.

"'I'm going to cum now,' I said. 'But you are not. Do you understand me? You are not going to cum yet. That's an order.'

"She moaned in response, but I could tell from how her breath quickened that she would obey me.

"I thrust up into her soft, wet flesh one final time and released my load of hot cum into her throbbing pussy.

"Then after a moment of pure pleasure, I moved out of her, leaving her wanting more.

"She gazed up at me wide-eyed. 'I...I need to cum, Jake. I need it so bad.' She was almost pleading.

"I smiled at her and stroked her face. 'Oh, sweetheart. I know. But that's not going to happen. Not now. Maybe not ever.'

Kelli was stunned. "So...did you ever? Did you finish what you started?"

Jake laughed. "Oh, perhaps. Perhaps not. Maybe I haven't quite made up my mind yet." He winked at Kelli.

Kelli felt like something about this last story was disturbing, but she couldn't quite put her finger on it. It seemed like something had caught her attention, just for a second, but it was gone now. She would have to think about it later. In the meantime, she wanted to hear more about Jake's history.

"So, you are experimenting with women now, but what about in the past? What happened after the twins and Marci?"

"Well, I didn't see a lot of women right away, not until after I had completely finished college and graduated. But, the threesome encounter I had with the Korean twins did prepare me somewhat for something that happened when I was back home and working in that lucrative IT job."

"Oh, really? What was that?"

"Basically, I developed a huge crush on the secretary, Melissa, who worked at the front desk. She was a typical Irish/Italian mix with green eyes and incredible blonde hair. She was very sensual and gorgeous, but cold as ice to me. I was infatuated and kept hitting on her over and over again for several weeks; I desperately wanted her to be my first girlfriend. She wouldn't give me the time of day, though, until one particular occasion."

Jake paused and took a sip of water. Kelli was intrigued. "Can you tell me more about that?"

He grinned at her. "You know, I like that about you. So inquisitive. And you try to be all professional about it."

She felt a little bit offended. "Uh, do you think that I'm not professional, Jake?"

He threw back his head and laughed outright. "Sure you are. You don't get off on hearing all of this at all, do you? Wait...of course you do."

She shook her head, unsure of how to respond. "No. No, I don't." It came out sounding weak.

"Oh yes, you do, you fox. You lap it up like a vixen drinks up milk.

You love it." His voice became soft, but firm at the same time. "I know it makes you wet."

Kelli felt like the session was spinning out of control. "So anyway, could you continue with your story?"

Jake smiled, but complied.

"It was a Friday, and Melissa and some of the other girls were going out for happy hour cocktails. I was only twenty at the time, but the place where she went was low-key place, so I was able to go with a friend. At happy hour, I kept hitting on her, but she still wouldn't give me the time of day. Her friend Linda, who also happened to be her roommate, was also in the group at the bar. She was a little bit different, not the typical look that I went for at that point."

"And what was that, exactly?" Kelli felt like it would be helpful to know what kind of women to whom Jake was attracted.

"Well, she was a brunette and I usually went for blondes, although I developed more of an attraction for brunettes later in life. In any case, Linda was attracted to me instantly and we hit it off and talked and talked and talked. At the end of the night, around 2:00 a.m., she asked me if I had to go home or if I could stay and spend some time with her. I told her that I didn't need to be anywhere right away, so she suggested that I come over to their place and hang out and talk more."

"How did Melissa react to that?"

"She actually seemed fine with it, and honestly, I was still a lot more interested in getting to know Melissa better than Linda. So all three of us went back to her apartment. Melissa went straight to her room, much to my disappointment. Linda and I sat together on the couch and started talking. I'd had a few drinks and was feeling horny, so then we started heavily making out and petting. After quite a while, she asked me, 'Do you want to do this?'

"I appreciated the fact that she had bothered to ask and told her yes, but also took the opportunity to let her know that I had had very few girlfriends in college, and wasn't all that experienced, other than with Marci, and the whentime before that with Elaine. She could tell, but she was very understanding and seemed to love the way I kissed and touched her."

"I'm sure she was impressed and touched by your honesty and transparency," commented Kelli. In fact, she was impressed, too. He was definitely authentic; she had to give him that.

"Yes, I think she was. In any case, eventually, she stood up from where we were sitting on the couch and drew me to my feet. She took me into her room which smelled absolutely amazing, like incense and warm skin.

"I was enthralled at this point, and couldn't wait to find out what Linda had in mind. She slowly pushed me back towards the bed, and then pushed me down so that I was lying on my back. She turned her back and I heard the sound of rustling. She turned toward me and I saw that she had drawn a long silk rope from a drawer and loosely tied me to her bed. It reminded me of Elaine, sending a pang through my heart, but I was highly aroused and found that I didn't mind at all.

"When I was bound and tied to the bedposts with the silken sash, Linda slowly and deliberately unbuttoned each button on my shirt and removed it. Then she started kissing up and down my body, kissing and caressing me slowly. She kissed down my chest, then my abs, and then down my thighs, teasing me mercilessly by avoiding my rock hard cock. When I could hardly stand it anymore she wrapped her wet mouth around my dick and started sucking me fiercely, making me harder."

Kelli gulped and held her voice steady through an act of sheer will. "Wow. Sounds...fun."

"Oh, it was. Linda went down on me for a good half hour at least.

139

When I was close to cumming, she suddenly stopped. She swung her leg over, climbed on top of me, and eased her naked hips down over my cock in reverse cowgirl position with her back to me. I was staring at her naked ass as she started riding me extremely hard, not so much bouncing up and down but more grinding into me, moving her hips in circles tight against my thighs and cock. I couldn't really move because I was tied up, so I just watched her from behind as her ass was grinding and wiggling on me. The sensation of her tight, wet pussy pressing down on my erect manhood was extremely intense and arousing.

"Linda carried on riding me, and just when I was about to explode inside her the door flew open and Melissa burst in. She was completely naked. She didn't even look at my shocked face, or my arms tied to the bed. She just simply asked Linda, 'Are you ready for me now?'

"Linda replied, 'Oh, yeah,' as Melissa came forward.

"Ready? Ready for what? What did she mean?"

"You'll see. The first thing she did was kneel at the foot of the bed. She then leaned in between mine and Linda's widely-spread legs. Linda arched her spine backward, thrusting her pelvis to the front and then Melissa started going down on both of us at the same time. First, she licked my balls and shaft, wrapping her tongue around my cock and flicking it up and down. Then I felt her move on, licking Linda's soaking wet, slippery pussy. All this time, I was still thrusting deep inside of Linda, even while Melissa was alternating between sucking and licking Linda and me. I couldn't see, but I could tell from Linda's moans that Melissa was licking and sucking her clit ferociously. Linda started rocking on top of me faster and faster, getting louder and louder."

Kelli was feeling extremely aroused herself by this point. She squirmed in her chair. Her arousal was strong enough that she could smell it and she wondered if Jake could, too. "So, uh, how long did this all go on?"

"This went on for twenty to forty minutes." Jake grinned at her.

Kelli had to ask the obvious question. "OK…and you lasted for that whole time?"

Jake's smile got wider. "Well, yeah, but don't get me wrong…it took all I had for me not to cum. They even commented on it, asking me how I was managing to last. In between thrusts, I told them that a previous girlfriend (Marci) had trained me well and that I shouldn't cum until the girl I was with had orgasmed two or three times. In fact, Marci was so demanding that she used to make me wait; she'd bring me to the very brink of orgasm, then wind me back down just to tease me again. When she was finally ready for me, she would demand that I cum on her body several times. If I didn't do this, she would punish me.

"In any case, I digress. Eventually, Linda's entire body spasmed as she came to a screaming climax. I was finished holding back, so I simultaneously came very heavily inside her. My energy was spent after that, but I was allowed to watch as Linda rolled off of me and went down on Melissa. Melissa stood with one hand braced against the wall and another holding a fistful of Linda's hair. As she wrapped one of her legs around Linda's neck and lifted her juicy ass and pussy up to her lover's mouth greedily, she began moaning loudly.

"Melissa came at least eight times while Linda avidly ate her out. When they were finally finished, they unbound me and lay cuddled up next to me on the rumpled bed for a while. I was feeling very satisfied sexually, but had enough of my wits about me to also be very confused about what had just transpired. I asked Melissa, 'You're obviously attracted to me, so why haven't you responded to my advances? Why is this only happening now?'

"I don't blame you," said Kelli. "I'm confused, too. What did they say in response?"

"Well, to my surprise, they both started to giggle. 'You still don't get it, do you?' asked Linda.

"'Get what?' Melissa was doubled over laughing now. She couldn't even talk because she was giggling so hard, and Linda was struggling to control her laughter as well. 'Get what?' I repeated. I was starting to feel a little bit angry.

"Linda was finally able to speak. 'Jake, you're so cute. Sorry to tell you this, but we're...well, if you hadn't noticed, we're both lesbians!' she told me, grinning. 'We don't generally pursue guys at all, but once in a while we get bored of just using toys and we bring home a male friend to play with us. It's like our...how do I put it...our special treat. It will probably never happen again with you, so don't take it the wrong way. Melissa and I are lovers. We're in a relationship.'

"I was quite surprised, but it all made sense. That's why Melissa had never looked my way or responded to my advances. Linda, however, was more on the bisexual side of the sexual spectrum and had given me a chance. In any case, together, the two of them gave me an amazing threesome experience."

Kelli had become even more turned on, but was curious. "How did you feel afterward?"

Jake cocked his head and looked at her for a while before answering, "Honestly? I felt hollow. I felt like the two of them had used me for their own purposes and there wasn't a lot of meaning or connection in it. Physically? Amazing. The experience of being with two beautiful women sexually is unrivalled, but it left me emotionally unsatisfied."

Kelli nodded. "Yes, I can see how you would feel like that. It seems like you are someone who really cares about having genuine connection with his partners. That's important."

"Yes. Extremely. That connection is the most important thing that two lovers can have. And that's probably why what happened with Mai Ling was so important."

"Mai Ling? Oh yes, you mentioned her during a previous session. She sounded significant in your life. Will you tell me about her?"

"Yes, I think the time is right to talk about Mai Ling. Mai Ling was my first real introduction into the world of online affairs."

"Really? How so?"

"Well, the incident that I just told you about, with Melissa and Linda…that was before I was married. But Mai Ling happened after I was married. Things weren't good between my wife and me, and I had put on a lot of weight and basically sunk into a depressive state. I was very out of shape at that time. I've already told you about how I first went on the affair website…do you remember?"

Kelli nodded. "Yes." How could she possibly forget?

"Well anyway, after I'd been on there for a few weeks, I was looking at profiles and suddenly got a message in my inbox. It was from Mai Ling. I checked out her profile, and saw a very petite, fit Asian woman. She wasn't necessarily my type, but her message was fun and flirty, so I replied. We struck up a conversation; she was smart, fun, and our conversation soon started to take an intensely sexual turn."

"How so?"

"Well, she asked me how big my cock was, for starters. And I obliged her by telling her, which really got her going."

Kelli must have had an intrigued look on her face because Jake paused, grinned, and winked at her. She felt flustered, and averted her eyes, looking down at the notepad in her lap.

"Uh, OK. So you were chatting with this woman, and then what happened?"

"Well, one thing led to another. She told me that it was her day off from work, and after chatting for a couple of hours, we made plans to meet for coffee. I was still unsure of myself at that point, but Mai Ling said that we should meet face to face to see if the chemistry that we'd discovered online was there in person."

"So you met?"

"Yes. We didn't live all that far away from each other, so she recommended a little coffee shop and we agreed to meet there. But when I got there, I had a little bit of a surprise."

"Oh, really? What was the surprise?"

"On her profile, she had appeared to be quite petite, and listed herself as five-foot-two and 115 pounds. In reality, she was closer to four-foot-ten and must have weighed about ninety-five pounds soaking wet. I was a little taken aback by the fact that she had fibbed, and that she was so tiny, but she was also very sexy. She was wearing a sleek, black satin, Asian-style skirt that was quite short and form-fitting, along with thigh-high black 'fuck-me' boots. She had a loose, peasant-style top on, and her hair was layered and fell along her shoulders and back. She was very attractive. She actually reminded me of my little butterfly, Tina…"

Jake's voice trailed off and he smiled.

Kelli asked, "Who was Tina?"

"Tina was the girl I took to my high school prom. My little butterfly.

"As I've mentioned before, I was quite a bit different from my peers throughout high school, and as a result I did not pursue women during those years as much as I did in later years.

"However, one very memorable experience did occur around that time; it involved my high school senior prom.

"Two weeks before the prom, all of my friends had found dates and I was left wondering if I'd be there by myself. One weekday afternoon, I went over to hang out with a good high school friend of mine, James. James was Asian-American, with a Chinese father and a Korean mother. We'd been buddies for a while. I also knew his older sister, Tina. She was a sophomore in college, and it just so happened that she was home for the weekend. I always had a little bit of a thing for Tina; she was petite, with long, dark hair and incredible dark, teardrop-shaped eyes.

"Since my experience with Elaine several years before, I had developed a definite taste for older women (a sexual preference that would last for many years, throughout my more submissive stage), and Tina had been the subject of my fantasies more than once. She often teased us after school, getting dressed to shop at the mall, prancing around in her underwear. However, I always respected my friendship with James and with Tina herself.

"That weekend, Tina asked me if I had a date to the prom and I told her that I didn't. To my surprise, she asked, 'Why don't you take me? I'd love to go with you!' I was delighted, although shocked. Little did I know that Tina was in the middle of an ugly breakup with her boyfriend; I found out long afterward that she had been in revenge mode, seeking jealousy from her ex-boyfriend, Richard.

"In any case, I accepted her offer gratefully. I didn't take it as any kind of sexual invitation because of my friendship with the family, but I was thrilled at the idea of hanging out with Tina. After the prom, it was the 'in' thing at that time for everyone to head down to the Jersey Shore and stay there for the whole weekend, drinking and having sexual adventures. I was still shy and reserved, but having Tina there was amazing, and we spent a lot of time just hanging out and talking, strolling on the beach, and walking the boardwalk at night, just the two of us. The long ride from my hometown to the shore would be something that would often occur in my life.

"Late one evening right before the weekend ended, Tina and I found ourselves in our room sprawled out on the bed playing the Chinese tile game Mahjong. Up to that point, we had shared a bed platonically, even though I had to be careful not to get noticeably aroused sleeping next to her every night. I even slept between the top sheet and cover so as to have a thin cotton layer between us. But this night was different. Tina and I began having some very intimate conversations about my time in high school, and my sexual experiences in particular.

"'So, have you ever been with a woman?' she asked me.

"'Well, uh, yeah. One so far.'

"She smiled at me. 'And? How was it? Did you enjoy that?'

"'I did...but I would like to have other experiences, too. That one was a little bit...odd.'

"Tina's eyes softened. Her eyes were vivaciously alive and intense, and really drew me in. I had the feeling she knew of the rumor of how I had lost my virginity.

"'Well, I can relate to things being awkward. Sexual stuff can be pretty taboo in Asian cultures, so there was a lot I had to learn too.'

"I was curious about her experiences, so I began asking her about Asian cultures and we talked for another hour or so. Tina was impressed by how much I knew about Chinese and Korean culture already, including saying basic phrases, such as 'Hello,' 'thank you,' and 'please.' She was equally impressed by my gaming skills and being able to pick up a penny with chopsticks, which all came from hanging out with her younger brother and parents after school.

"As the night went on, I noticed she got quieter and quieter and was just looking at me with those intense, dark, almond eyes. Eventually, she reached over and put her hand on my arm.

"'Jake, would you like me to demonstrate some Chinese massage techniques that I know?'

"I just nodded. We had both been drinking that night, more heavily than usual, and the sexual chemistry was definitely there between us. She leaned over me and started massaging my chest gently. She pushed me back, so that I was lying flat on the bed, and slowly unbuttoned my shirt. I was feeling very aroused and lifted my hand to stroke her face and play with her long hair a little. She softly grinned, pushed me back, and bent down, brushing the bare skin of my chest with her lips. Then suddenly, she opened her mouth wider and flicked my nipples with her little pink tongue. It felt absolutely amazing.

"Tina's massage and her tongue flicking my nipples were intensely arousing to me, but I suddenly became scared at the thought of damaging my friendships with her and her brother. I sat up a little and pushed her away gently.

"'Tina...I, I just don't know about this. It feels weird. I mean, I like you a lot and everything...but...," I trailed off.

"She smiled. 'What is it, Jake? Aren't you enjoying this?'

"'Well, yes...but we've had so much fun hanging out. I just don't want to ruin our friendship or anything.'

"Tina laughed. 'Oh, Jake. I really appreciate the fact that you would even think of that! You're so sweet! But don't worry about it. I like you too, and I value your friendship, but this doesn't have be anything more than a little bit of fun between the two of us. Are you cool with that? If you are, I am. I promise. I want you to see me as your little butterfly. Can I be your butterfly, just this once?'

"I couldn't resist, and simply laid back and pulled Tina's head over me. She bent down and started kissing me, slowly and passionately. Still being quite inexperienced, I let her lead, and she gently probed my mouth with her tongue, alternating between playing with my upper and lower lips with hers, nibbling softly.

"Tina then unzipped my jeans and drew out my cock. She gasped a little and her eyes widened as she took in my size. She stroked my shaft and teased me with her mouth a little, licking and sucking up and down my cock. I moaned and laid back, running my hands through her hair.

"Eventually, she drew back and suddenly stood up.

"'Where are you going?' I asked.

"She replied, 'I just need to get something out of my bag...' She went to her suitcase and drew out a long, silk scarf. She came back to the bed and began to wrap the scarf over my eyes. I stiffened a little, and she drew back.

"'Is everything OK? Do you mind if I blindfold you?'

"I was remembering Elaine. It wasn't that I minded so much; it just simply brought back a flood of intense memories.

"'Um...it's OK. It just reminds me of something. Can you just not use them so I can watch you enjoy me?'

"Tina smiled again; her eyes were soft and inviting.

"'We don't need to use it then,' she whispered. With that, she lay the scarf aside, straddled me, and eased herself down over my rock hard cock. I was so hard that my cock was throbbing, aching almost painfully. Her pussy around me was slick, smooth, and incredibly tight. She started rocking back and forth, slowly and surely, leaning forward a little with her hands on my chest.

"'Oh fuck, you feel so good,' she said softly. 'So thick and hard. Why don't you have a girlfriend? This makes no sense...' I knew what she meant, but she didn't understand how parents always chastised their daughters for even knowing me. If you weren't Irish-

American or Italian, you were the minority in town, as was she, being Asian. Fortunately for her, her father owned the only Chinese restaurant in the area and was well liked. What would her ultraconservative parents think of me and her?

"I'm not even sure how long we stayed in that position, but I know it was a while. Tina took things slow, but I remember watching her face shift and change as she began to move towards her climax. It took her quite some time to take all of me inside her, and I watched the slightly pained expression as she pushed to take me in deeper. She pressed herself against me avidly, hungrily. But she did something that was new to me: She looked deep into my eyes and held eye contact. This made the entire sexual experience much more intense and meaningful.

"Tina was getting closer and closer to cumming, moving wildly back and forth, and up and down my shaft, grinding her clit against me. 'Fuck, you are a keeper...,' she softly gasped out. 'Don't fucking cum, yet. I need to cum. Please, please just stay hard; I really, really need this,' she demanded. Just then, Tina rocked forward in one final push and clenched around me in climax, digging her perfectly manicured nails deep into my back. I let myself go as I thrust upwards into her, and the rush of pleasure came to the two of us simultaneously. We both cried out loudly. Tina stayed on top and kept me inside her for a few more minutes as she slumped forward, pressing her face into my neck. She finally drew herself off and curled up next to me. We laid there for what seemed like hours, just holding each other, not saying a word. It was very intimate and sweet; we both knew that we could never be together.

"That wasn't our only time together, as we stayed friends and kept in touch for many years afterwards. Her rocky relationship with Richard went on and off, often with months being apart, and it wouldn't be uncommon for Tina to page me with 612 during her down times (as cell phones came about, she would text me the same), the date I was labeled her butterfly, for a butterfly session. She knew I didn't sleep around, and our sessions were always mind blowing, always ending with her head on my chest, just wondering.

Later, she even got a butterfly tattoo on her hip, and I knew what it meant. With Tina, my little butterfly, I got my first taste of what intimacy and passion could really be. I will never forget her for that reason."

Kelli asked, "Did you keep in touch with her?"

"Well, after our prom experience we remained friends and hung out a lot with her brother at her house. I would see her boyfriend, Richard, from time to time. Eventually, he became her fiancé. But whenever they were on the rocks and having trouble, Tina would call me up and we would get together for sex. This happened on several occasions. However, it got kind of complicated because she and Richard eventually got married. Believe it or not, I was invited to Richard's bachelor party, and I saw something there that really disturbed me."

"Oh?" asked Kelli. "What was that?"

"Well, I saw Richard having raw, unprotected sex with a hooker. The prostitute was a complete stranger. I couldn't believe it. Tina was so fragile, so sweet. I was incredibly disgusted with Richard's actions. I really went back and forth, trying to decide if I should tell her about it or not. I knew that they really loved each other and I didn't know if I wanted to get in the middle of that. It was a major dilemma."

"So what did you do?"

"I stayed quiet. I knew how she felt about him and I didn't want to take anything away from her. I just couldn't do it. Even after they got married, we stayed friends. Even after their marriage, whenever they had rocky times, she would call me. She hated how *mechanical* he was during sex—never adventurous, always doing the same things—and loved the sex that we had—the stamina, the oral. I started becoming her sexual outlet."

"Wow," said Kelli, "That's really special. Did you have any other experiences with women who were good friends?"

"Yes," Jake said, "During my career in IT, one of my main clients would often send me to his home to make sure that the home computer was connecting into the office network. He had been married once before, a story for another time, but was now remarried. His new wife was often at the house when I was fixing the computer network there. One day, I was working in the office and I noticed a photograph that was beautifully framed next to the computer. In it, there was an incredibly attractive woman with a great smile. I asked my client's wife, 'Who is that?' She told me that it was her sister.

"Intrigued, I asked if her sister was seeing anyone. With a laugh, she replied, 'Oh, she's single, but I'm not sure that you're her type.' And with that, she winked at me and walked away. At that point, I really wasn't sure what she meant by that. I was slightly hurt by her blunt statement, but I just let it go.

"Three or four weeks later, my client asked me to set up another computer, this time at his office building. He told me it was for a new company employee. Imagine my surprise when I walked in and saw the girl from the photo! The new employee was his wife's gorgeous sister.

"I couldn't help but strike up a conversation with her, and discovered that she was as personable as she was beautiful. However, as we chatted, I started looking around her office and had a startling realization. All of the art on the walls and the books on the shelves gave something away. It slowly dawned on me: She was gay! The dead giveaway was the gay pride flag that she proudly pinned on her corkboard. That is what her sister had meant by 'not her type.'

"Fortunately I realized this fact in time to keep from making a fool of myself, and Kara and I actually really hit it off. Starting that day, we developed a close friendship and would often spend time together after work shopping at the mall, getting lunch, talking about our dates, and even partying at clubs in Manhattan.

"After three or four years of friendship, while Kara was in a serious relationship with another woman, she and I decided to go to a particular club in the city. At the club, people were playing with glow sticks, the type that you can wear around your neck and smaller ones that people passed around orally. Some of the girls, including Kara and her girlfriend, started passing around tiny glow sticks with their teeth. All the girls involved were other lesbians who knew Kara. The game of passing the glow sticks was just between them, leaving me out of it. I would slowly tiptoe my way to the bar as they flirted with each other. But as the night went on, we got more and more drunk, and then Kara levitated towards me and surprised me by passing a glow stick to me with her mouth, kissing me in the process. This happened a few different times, and initially I wrote it off as drunken friendly fun. The final time Kara passed the stick to me, she actually kissed me more passionately and with a little bit of tongue. She then nibbled on my bottom lip. It was obvious to me that something more was going on.

"To avoid hurting our tight friendship, I excused myself from the group and made my way to the club's unisex bathroom. It was a large forty-foot-by-eighty-foot room with urinals on one side and stalls on the other. Drugs were prevalent in the club; E or X, or even cocaine were often at the site. I never used the urinals, as gay men would often look over and make you feel uncomfortable, so I waited in line to use a stall. I entered one, urinated, cleaned myself, and turned around to exit the stall, only to find a short, drunk girl staring at me. She snuck into the stall with me and said, 'I've been watching you all night dancing with those hot girls. I want to suck you. Pull your pants back down and let's fuck now in the stall.'

"I smiled, and said, 'Listen, ummm, I'm gay, we are all just hanging out having a good time. Is that OK?'

"I don't know why I said that, as Kara's kiss was still fresh on my mind.

"'You ARE gay?! How can you turn this down?' she proclaimed in great disbelief.

"Indeed, she was hot—great body and beautiful hair, skin, and eyes...but, just to fuck me like that, without knowing me was a big turn-off. I pushed her drunk-ass aside, kissed her on the forehead, and said, 'Listen. There are a ton of guys here and I'm sure someone will want his dick sucked, just not me.'

"I exited the stall, and as soon as I left, Kara was standing right outside just looking and laughing at me, nodding her head.

"On our way home, I shared a cab with Kara and several other girls back to Hoboken, NJ, where I had left my car to drive everyone home. We dropped the girls off one by one and she and I were left alone together in the car. When we arrived at Kara's house, she looked over at me and gave me that look, that special look, that 'fuck-me face' we all joke about. I recognized it immediately.

"'Jake, you are all over the road. Come inside; the alcohol is hitting you hard,' she whispered in her drunk voice, holding my wrist.

"'I love you as a friend; you have been amazing to me and I don't want to lose you.'

"I was unbelievably shaky, and sheer butterflies ripped through me. We were both heavily drunk, and both had an attraction to one another. My mind told me to leave, but my heart told me to stay. I paused and stared into her eyes; I knew I had to say something smooth soon.

"As Kara invited me into her house, I was suspicious of her motives. I suspected she wanted more.

"When we went inside the house, things got intense. She poured us both some wine and we started chatting. I told her about some of my sexual history, including the stories of Elaine and Tina. I had mentioned Elaine to her before, but Kara was a great listener and this time I went into more detail about my experiences.

"I wanted her to open up too, so I asked her when she had known that she was a lesbian and that she didn't like men.

"Kara said that when she was younger she had experimented with her sexuality. She had spent some time on a rich man's yacht, boating along the Jersey Shore in the summer.

"At the time, she was the only woman on board, with several young guys in their twenties.

"'What were they like?' I asked.

"'Oh, they were mostly really good guys. Young, fit, and hot. I liked almost all of them except for one. He was a real asshole. I could smell it on him.'

"'So what happened?'

"'I agreed to have group sex with three of the guys, the ones I really liked. But the fourth man, the one I really despised, decided to force himself into the group sex. We were all pretty drunk, but I was still really clear about not wanting to be with him. I specifically told the extra guy that I didn't want him to participate or to have sex with me in any way.' Kara's eyes were full of pain as she told the story, so I put my arm around her.

"'So he didn't listen?'

"'No. It…it ended up being something very similar to a gang rape, because the other men—the guys who I thought were my friends—didn't stop the other guy from being part of the sex act. I was telling them no but was basically forced to have sex with all of them at the same time.'

"I was really shocked and sad for her, but I asked her why she hadn't fought back and tried to wrestle her way out of the situation. Kara was a tall, sturdy girl; she was extremely athletic and could take on most guys.

"'Oh yeah?' she asked, 'You think I should have wrestled my way out?'

"'Uh huh,' I nodded.

"'Kinda like this...?' Smiling, Kara grabbed me and started wrestling with me. We fell back onto her couch.

"I realized where things were going. 'Kara, I need to tell you something.'

"She pulled back. 'What?'

"'This reminds me of my first threesome experience. That was also with a lesbian—two, actually. And honestly, I kind of felt used. I don't think that we should have sex unless it's really meaningful.'

"Kara was surprised, but agreed with me. She brought out some bedding and set up the couch for me to sleep on.

"In the morning, I was amazed to wake up and find that my hands had been bound above my head and a blindfold had been placed over my eyes. I could smell Kara's perfume and feel her stroking my abs.

"'Kara...this feels amazing, but like I told you, I don't want to do anything unless it's meaningful.'

"She whispered in my ear, 'Oh, this will be meaningful, Jake. You're the first guy I've been with who really respected me.'

"I felt a little nervous. 'Should we use a safe word or something?'

"She laughed a little. 'No. This is going to be so amazing. I am going to fuck you so good that we won't need a safe word.'

"She proceeded to go down on me, making my cock stiff by licking

155

and sucking me with her mouth and lips before she climbed on top of me and rode me to climax. She did other things to me that I could never put into words…it was incredible. She had made her own line of candles called **Pride Candel**. She took out one of them and proceeded to drip hot wax on my body, along my chest, down to my waist, torso, cock, and balls, often quietly giggling at my pain. At the end, she released my hands, but kept me blindfolded, head resting on my chest, hands caressing me. I held her firmly; we both knew this was a night, a moment, never to be spoken about in public.

"We stayed great friends afterwards, often hanging out and joking around with each other. We never really talked about it, but I knew we would never be together again sexually, and she told me on several occasions that if she ever chose to be with a guy again, it would be me.

"I want to finish telling you about Mai Ling."

"OK. You told me what she was wearing. What were you wearing at this point?"

"I had thrown on my ripped jeans and a V-neck tee. I wanted to look nice for her, of course, but also wanted to keep the casual vibe going."

"Makes sense. So what happened when you met?"

"Well, we really hit it off. She was very aggressive and sexual. She started touching me almost immediately, laying her hand on my arm and then along my leg as we talked.

"After an hour or so, she asked, 'Do you want to go sit in the car and make out? I really want to kiss you.'

"'Oh yeah? And why is that?' I grinned at her.

"'Hmmm…maybe because I think you are cute, and we've been having great conversation? Also…I can't stop thinking about our sexy chats online. I feel like there is a spark between us. Being near you makes me horny.'

"I was flattered and also found Mai Ling attractive, so I was happy to comply.

"'Sure! Sounds like a great idea.'

"We went out to the car and she was like a tiger; she literally jumped into my lap and started kissing me ferociously. It had been so long since I'd experienced that level of passion that my mind was blown. It felt amazing. Her hands were roaming everywhere, and when she came to the bulge in my jeans she groaned with pleasure and anticipation. I could tell that she wanted to see it and hold it, but I held back at that time. We kept kissing and heavily petting for an hour or so, then Mai Ling drew back from me and spoke.

"'Damn, you're hot. I bet you're an incredible fuck.' She smiled and pushed her hair back from her forehead. Her eyes were bright and full of desire.

"I smiled back at her, gazing into her eyes, and stroked her inner thigh. 'The reports I get back are good,' I chuckled. 'I've also had some excellent teachers.' I remembered Marci, and Tina.

"'And from what I can tell, it feels like your cock is pretty fucking big.' Mai Ling was definitely blunt and straightforward.

"I shrugged. 'Yes, you could say that.' I paused. 'Want to see?'

"Her eyes lit up like a Christmas tree and she nodded eagerly.

"Slowly, I unzipped my pants and drew out my swollen cock for her to admire. She gasped when she saw it.

"'Oh my God. Yes. That is what I'm talking about. Holy fuck, that is gorgeous!'

"Her face was full of lust. She said, 'Let's go to your house and fuck now. I need you. Bad.'

"I was a little taken aback by her suggestion to go to my house. I wasn't sure what she meant.

"'Uh, my house? Why would we want to go there?'

"She leaned in close to me, and nibbled my earlobe for a second before murmuring, 'I want to fuck you in your bed. I'm going to fuck you like you've never been fucked before.'

"I was puzzled. 'Uh, why? I mean, why does it need to be in my bed? There's a hotel near here. Can't we go there?'

"Mai Ling shrugged. 'I just want to. I like fucking men in their beds at home. It gives me a buzz, knowing that I'm fucking them in the place where they usually sleep with their wives. Call me crazy, but it's just what I like.'

"This shocked me to my core, and I drew back a little. It didn't feel right to me. I might not have had the best relationship with my wife, but fucking another woman in our marital bed just wasn't acceptable to me. It was too disrespectful.

"I shook my head. 'No, sorry. I can't do that. It's just not something I want to do. But why don't we go to your place instead?'

"Now it was Mai Ling's turn to shake her head. 'Huh uh. Nope. Can't do it.'

"'Why not?'

"She just shrugged. 'I just don't bring guys back to my place. It's kind of a rule I have.' She cocked her head sideways and twisted a piece of hair around her finger. 'So…what's it going to be then? C'mon! Let's go to your place. You know you want to! I've gotta have that mammoth cock inside me. You're killing me, Jake!'

"I held firm. 'No, I'm serious. I won't do that. So why don't we go to a hotel? It would be a shame to miss out on this connection just because we couldn't find a place to go, wouldn't it?'

"Mai Ling finally agreed. We checked into a local hotel around the corner, and started making out on the bed right away. Again I was blown away by how passionate and wild she was; she bit my neck and my lower lip, and drove her long nails into my back. For such a small thing, she was incredibly forceful and energetic.

"She practically tore my clothes off and raked her nails down my bare chest, pausing only when she reached my groin. She moaned again, stroking the length of my shaft, running her long nails lightly over my balls.

"'You like it, then?' I asked.

"'God, yes! I need it, babe. Come here.'

"She lay back on the bed and opened her legs. I could see how aroused and swollen her pussy was, glistening with juices. I gently guided myself into her, but because she was so petite, I could only get about half of my cock inside her. She was so small and tight that it was almost painful for me, and not terribly satisfying.

"She, on the other hand, was moaning and almost screaming with pleasure. After just a few thrusts, she climaxed for the first time, bucking and pitching herself upwards.

"'More!' she shouted. 'Give me more of that rock solid cock! I want more!' I pushed in another inch or so, and she shrieked as another orgasm swept over her. It was actually quite uncomfortable for me sexually. My first affair wasn't going quite how I had planned."

Kelli was listening intently, and seized on this comment. "That's interesting. How did you feel emotionally?" Here was a chance to steer them into safer waters, waters that didn't make her want to strip naked and impale herself on his lap.

"Emotionally, I felt fine. It was nice to get some form of relief after having been starved of sex for so long. I was mostly just trying to find some physical pleasure. In the end, I didn't actually come inside of Mai Ling. She was too tight. She orgasmed six or seven times though, and then she let me ejaculate over her stomach when she was through."

Kelli looked down at her notes and then back up at Jake.

"So, why was Mai Ling so important then? It sounds like you had fun, but I guess I don't quite understand why she has such significance in your journey."

Jake sat up a little bit straighter. "Ah! Right. The reason that Mai Ling is so important isn't because of the sex we had. No, there is a much bigger reason. That day that we met up and went to the hotel for sex, I was much, much more overweight and out of shape than how you see me now. I had basically lost my confidence and sense of pride in my appearance. But Mai Ling helped me change that."

"Really? How?"

"That day, after we had sex and were lying in bed she said, 'You know, Jake. You're really not a bad looking guy. There's a lot of potential here.'

"I wasn't sure how to take that, so I replied, 'What do you mean by potential?'

"'Well, I already told you on my profile that I'm a personal trainer at the gym. I see guys like you, and I think, *Wow! If he just worked out, he could have any woman he wanted!* And that's the truth. You COULD have any woman you wanted if you were willing to put in the work and get fit.'

"I pretended to be offended. 'What, so I'm not cute now?' Mai Ling just giggled and ran her hand over my chest and stomach.

"'No, silly. That's my point. You ARE cute, but this could be a lot more toned and defined. Then you'd be incredibly hot.'

"I was intrigued. 'So, since you're a trainer, what do you recommend?'

"'I'll tell you what,' said Mai Ling, 'Why don't you let me give you a few training sessions? Come by the gym tomorrow and we'll get you started!'

"And that is what happened. Things didn't work out sexually between me and Mai Ling, but she became my personal trainer for a while. Because of her, I started to get my confidence back and really got back into shape. I owe that to her."

Once again, Kelli was impressed. "Wow! That's an amazing story. And how did she take it when you told her that you weren't going to continue as lovers?"

"Oh, she was fine. She had plenty to choose from. She did tell me that I had been one of the best, though. She couldn't stop talking about my large penis for a while, but eventually we really were just friends and she put me through my paces at the gym like nobody else. After she was finished with me, I was a completely different person."

"I can imagine," said Kelli. Jake's transformation was incredibly inspiring for her. She imagined doing something similar, changing her life around.

At that moment, there was a knock on her office door. It was her secretary. "Uh, Kelli? There's a delivery for you."

Kelli wasn't expecting anything, so she was confused. "Bring it in," she said. Turning to Jake, she asked, "You don't mind, do you?"

He grinned. He looked excited, somehow. "No, I don't mind at all. By all means, see what your delivery is."

His tone suddenly made Kelli feel suspicious. "Wait a minute...is this...this isn't...have you sent me something?"

Jake just kept grinning. At that moment, the secretary brought in a huge box and set it down next to Kelli, then left, closing the door behind her.

Jake gazed at her with those intense eyes. "Go on, Kelli. Open it."

She carefully pried open the cardboard container and gasped at what she saw. Inside was a beautifully carved wooden box, with intricate designs all around it.

Jake immediately took out a small pocket measuring tape, and a packet of organic honey from his pocket. "Fifty-two by thirty-one by thirty-one inches. *Perrrrfect,*" Jake said as he measured the box.

"This is from you...?" she stammered.

He stood up and walked over to her. She could smell him and feel the heat from his body.

"Yes, it's from me. Do you know what this is, Kelli?"

She shook her head. "Tell me."

"Promise me, Kelli, that from now on, you will keep all of your sexual toys in this box. Your vibrators, your plugs, your nipple clamps, your handcuffs. All of it. It goes in here, in the sacred box."

Kelli looked up at him. "But...but I don't even have..." She was trying to tell him that she didn't even own half of the toys he had just mentioned. But as she was trying to speak, he leaned forward and placed his finger against her lips. He opened the small packet of organic honey, dipped his finger into it, and spread it evenly across her lips.

"Shhhhhh, Kelli. Don't argue. You will have all of these things in good time. I intend to teach you." Jake reached over and pulled her head closer, and passionately kissed her honey-dripped lips.

She stared up at him, feeling herself get wet. Thoughts of his domination swept over her whole body, making her nipples perk up and her pussy get juicier and juicier.

"Teach me what, Jake?" she whispered.

He leaned forward, close to her ear: "Everything."

Then he took a step back. "Oh, and one more thing, Kelli."

She looked at him and waited for him to speak.

"From now on, there is a new rule. You will call me, Sir."

ABOUT THE AUTHOR

Jake Furie Lapin is a writer, entrepreneur, wine drinker, and coffee addict based in New Jersey. Jake's writings aim to explore sexuality and sensuality, including the BDSM lifestyle, through the beauty of the written word. The Spice of Life is his first novel. He has also published a periodical, Jake's Chronicles, a journal of the everyday life of Jake Furie Lapin, with continuations of his blogs, recipes, reviews, and more. Jake encourages all of his readers and fans to explore his website and check out his blog @ www.tsolbook.com. The Contact Me page has links to all his social media accounts. Let him know your thoughts through your comments and feedback.

Made in the USA
Lexington, KY
05 December 2017